TEMPT THE OCEAN

A Slightly Dark Romance

Agnès de Savigny

ISBN 978-0-9949532-1-6 (Paperback Edition)
ISBN 978-0-9949532-0-9 (Electronic Edition)

This is a work of fiction. Names, characters, places, and incidents either are the products of the author's imagination or are used fictitiously. Any resemblance to actual events, locales, or persons, living or dead, is entirely coincidental.

Second Printing, 2019

PO Box 15326
Queensway High PO
Toronto, On
M8Y 0B4

Visit somatime.wordpress.com/agnes-de-savigny/#Agnes

For Dianna, who asked me to write her a story while I sailed the Atlantic.

Acknowledgements

Special thanks to Paula Tiberius for the editorial feedback and enthusiastic tips on getting a novel out the door. Special thanks also to Jo Karaplis for the copy editing and further enthusiasm. Thanks to Connie Kaneko for her early copy editing. And to everyone else who has contributed to helping me find the right title.

On a personal note, I'd like to thank my sister Carolyn for calling me a writer before I called myself one, and Aaron for never considering that I wasn't.

TEMPT THE OCEAN

Chapter 1

I studied the crack on my ceiling as if the weight of the day depended on how well I knew each turn of the crooked line. The fibres of the carpet I lay on left their impression in the back of my head, making my scalp itch. I could have—should have—gotten up ages ago to do something with my day. But I had given up on myself months ago.

A phone call from my uncle Bill interrupted my eternal moment of self-pity.

"We need another person on board to make the crossing comfortable," urged Bill, who with his second wife Margaret was about to set sail across the Atlantic in their forty-two foot yacht. I had sailed with them a few times and knew their boat. They wanted me to get a flight to Spain in order to sail back with them.

"Tell her we'll have to take an ad out otherwise," Margaret shouted in the background. I could hear a sea-do humming in the distance.

"We'd rather have you join us than someone we don't know," said Bill.

"I'd love to, but I really don't think I can take the time," I lied. I had no way of paying for a trip to Europe. I should be focusing on looking for work—one of these days.

"That's not what we heard."

Ouch.

"Bill," shouted Margaret again, this time closer to the phone and trying to disguise her voice in a bad imitation of a whisper. "Did you tell her we'll pay her way? You know she doesn't have any money."

"I'm guessing you heard that," said Bill.

"I did, Uncle Bill. That's very generous, but I don't feel right taking your money."

"We can cover *your* expenses, or we can find some ass online and pay *his*. I'd rather pay you—at least I know you can sail."

A change of scenery—gorgeous never-ending ocean—could be the kick in the pants I needed to get my life back on track. A perfect storm of betrayal had crushed both my self-reliance and my self-respect. I had never seen myself as someone who would fall apart over a man, but it had happened. And now I was letting that betrayal deny me an all-expenses paid trip across the ocean. Well, no more. I told Bill I would join them.

"Good," replied Bill. "Because I already bought you a plane ticket. Your flight leaves on Friday."

***

I arrived at the airport in Gran Canaria after dark. I found the sudden tropical heat exhausting after an already tiring three-connection flight. Bill and Margaret—dressed in their typical yacht-cruising gear of printed t-shirts, shorts, Teva sandals and dime store sunglasses—embraced me as I emerged from the arrival gate, bags in tow. Their generosity and the humid air permeated my heart with the first warmth I'd felt in months.

I was too excited to fall asleep during the long drive to the marina at the south tip of Gran Canaria. Bill and Margaret had moored their boat *Quixotic* at a resort development built around an old fishing village named Puerto de Mogan. We entered the marina at a slow crawl, following the road along a narrow spit which hugged the harbour. I tried to make out the boat in her slip as we parked the car. Lights glinted off every surface in the marina, making it difficult to distinguish one boat from the next. Finally I saw her, tied to a floating dock and almost hidden by a 60 ft monstrosity in the adjacent slip.

Quixotic was a good-looking yacht, tastefully outfitted in a palette of ivory, forest green, and teak. She boasted two sleeping cabins, a small galley, a lounge area, and a modern navigation station below. A four foot prow jutted out at her nose, the perfect perch for dolphin-watching. The yacht's modest but comfortable cockpit faced us at the stern with an invitation to come on board and relax.

The big yacht which overshadowed Bill and Margaret's demanded more attention. Covered head to toe in bright brass fittings, her sleek shape reeked of opulent wealth. Her owner's choice to moor her bow first, unlike every other yacht in the marina, compounded the boat's arrogant flamboyance by further diminishing the stature of the boats alongside her. I concluded that the boat belonged to a wealthy retiree on his second—or fourth—marriage, who pined for the days of bossing around his minions.

Bill, Margaret, and I shuffled my heavy bags from the trunk of the rental car along the floating dock to the boat. I had thought the floating dock balancing act was tricky until I saw our access to the cockpit. A narrow plank attached to the stern jutted out just above the precarious dock, rolling in slow motion with the movement of the boat in the water. We were going to have to carry everything over the 12-inch wide moving ramp without dropping anything into the water below.

A fierce yapping erupted from the depths of the large yacht next to us, startling me as I balanced my way, heavy suitcase in hand, across the tippy gangplank. The furious fifteen-pound fur-ball that emitted the aching noise pollution swept from the unlit stern to the point along the high deck right above our heads. I could hear the footsteps of the dog's owner racing to quiet him, but the damage was done. I felt myself lean too far in one direction and stuck my arm out blindly for a handhold that wasn't there. I was going to fall in the water and ruin any semblance of comfort all because some fat female cruiser wearing loud aqua shorts and a loose t-shirt printed with the name of some obscure port couldn't control her stupid lapdog.

My uncle caught my elbow and steadied me.

I nodded him a grateful thank you before turning my glare up to the female cruiser.

But the figure my stink-eye landed on did not belong to an

over-the-hill retiree. The shape silhouetted by the glinting marina lights belonged to a young, tall, and very fit man. And rather than the typical tight-shorts-and-loose-tee outfit of a female cruiser, he wore a pair of loose nylon swim shorts and no shirt at all.

"Obelix!" he said to the dog as he swept up the offensive rag in his rugged arms. The deep tone of his voice resonated with a hint of embarrassment.

"He is adopted—a stray," said the sailor to us, by way of apology. He spoke with a soft French accent. His dishevelled dark hair hinted that he'd just been sleeping. He smiled as he spoke. He admonished the dog, who responded by licking the Frenchman's unshaven chin. The adorable scene melted my wrath.

While Bill casually introduced us, identifying me as his niece, rather than by name, I discreetly checked out my new French acquaintance named Xavier. I considered the possibility that this sexy man might be the son of the filthy rich retiree and his pudgy fourth wife, but concluded that more likely he was someone they'd hired to babysit the boat while they were away. Xavier carried himself with a relaxed confidence. The shadows obscured the details of his features, but I could see a long straight nose bracketed by tall cheek bones which rose above the stubble of his three-day growth. His eyes sparkled in the magical light of the Marina. His skin had the tone of a Mediterranean who spent all his waking hours kissed by the sun.

I didn't know what to say after the brief introduction and Xavier remained silent following his polite "hello." Bill and Margaret said nothing either, as though they were standing aside to let the young people strike up a conversation. My uncle broke the awkward pause by wishing our neighbour goodnight and continuing with my luggage into the belly of *Quixotic*. I glanced back at the adjacent deck in time to catch our hot neighbour's gaze as he did the same. He winked and disappeared into the dark with his dog.

I followed my uncle and aunt down *Quixotic*'s steep wooden ladder into the cabin below. They had arranged a cozy bed for me in the aft cabin, a closet-sized bunk tucked under the cockpit. I fell asleep the moment my head hit the pillow, my dreams unblemished by devastating images for the first time since finding my man in bed with my best friend.

***

The dry rocky hills of the Gran Canaria rose above the resort, barren and imposing. The only greenery was that which had been artificially transplanted from other tropical locations by the developers. There wasn't much left of the original fishing village of Puerto de Mogan except a small fleet of run-down trawlers docked at the end of the marina. The villagers still lived here, but most were employed in the service of the development. Their cats were here too, and lined the jetty waiting for hand-outs from fishermen and sailors.

Bill warned me that there wouldn't be much time to see anything of Gran Canaria. He was anxious to get sailing after determining that we must leave the next day in order to arrive in Antigua for Christmas. We had one day to complete all of our departure tasks before the three weeks at sea—buy groceries and last minute gear, pick up laundry, secure the boat, and prepare the departure paperwork. I ran off to find a sun hat while Bill and Margaret took the car to collect their last load of laundered clothing.

Between departure chores we ate our meals at the boardwalk cafes which lined the marina development's canals. The developers had chosen the name Little Venice for the marina and its handful of hotels, but the place was overrun with German tourists. The Little Venetian canal-side cafes served more schnitzel than pasta.

After lunch we returned to the boat with a car full of groceries. We found our hot French neighbour showering in his Speedo in front of *Quixotic*, using a hose provided on the dock. There wasn't much about him that could be left to the imagination. Not that I could imagine anything much better. I tried not to stare at him as I approached with my bags full of produce. He caught my eye as I passed, so I grasped for something clever (and casual) to say…

"That's a rather large ship you have," I blurted. Ugh! I kept moving, hoping that he couldn't hear me through the sound of the running water.

"Uh, merci," he hesitated through his soapy lather. He added, in an almost inaudible murmur, "Those are rather nice melons."

I fought a grin as I balanced my way across the wobbly plank with the groceries. His melon line was worse than mine! And much more offensive. Or was it? I stole a glance back at him as I stepped safely into the cockpit. He was watching me through the spray of the hose as he rinsed his hair out. He smiled but then turned away.

Bill orchestrated the final touches for our departure during the afternoon by putting Margaret and I to work right up until dinner time. We stowed away or tied down any loose articles on the boat. We discarded the last of Bill and Margaret's garbage. There was some disagreement between Bill and Margaret about what might be garbage, but Margaret won those arguments in the end. Bill decided his chrome needed cleaning, one last time.

We headed back along the spit to the German Schnitzel houses for dinner after the afternoon of deck scrubbing and rope coiling. Bill was a tough taskmaster. He didn't take it too well when Margaret and I joked about mutiny before we'd even started the ocean voyage. The tension eased with the first glass of wine.

The dock had grown quiet by the time we returned later that evening. No shaggy lapdog attacked us as we giggled our tipsy way across the floating plank. No sexy Frenchman peered down at us with sleepy eyes. My disappointment surprised me.

Bill and Margaret went to bed early. Their slumbering noises crept from the V-berth in the bow through the cabin and up into the cockpit where I huddled, trying to stave off boredom. I gave up and pretty soon I made myself cozy in my little aft-cabin. I read for a short while, and then turned the light off. In the quiet darkness I could hear the faint sounds of groovy electronica floating across from the big yacht next door. It was very soothing, and in conjunction with the slow rhythms of the boat in the water, the music gently rocked me to sleep.

***

In the morning everything that we had stowed away or secured the day before had to be double-checked according to Bill's inspection before we left. I figured out how to make coffee with a stove-top espresso maker on the gimballed gas stove. Margaret put away the last of our groceries and checked her e-mail via short-wave radio. Bill had gone to the Marina office to register our departure and was taking longer than expected. I decided to take advantage of the extra time by squeezing in a quick shower before we set sail.

I grabbed my towel, toiletries, and a change of clothes. I shut the little door to the aft cabin behind me as I left the boat and shouted to Margaret that I was going. I got no response from the boat's head where she was brushing her teeth, but I assumed she could hear me.

The communal marina showers were only a short walk away from our floating dock, housed in a small building at the head of the spit. I wanted to be sure I was really clean, knowing it might be awhile before I had the chance to shower again. I took a long time washing my hair—maybe too long. I dried myself off with the towel, and pulled shorts on over a bikini—good sailing wear. I gathered everything up when I was done, wrapping my dirty clothes in my wet towel, and hurrying back to the boat before I got yelled at for holding up the 'schedule'.

But the boat was gone.

Chapter 2

I stood at the end of the empty slip, staring at the water lapping through the space where the boat should have been. I was barely conscious of the wet towel bundled in one hand, or the wet toiletry bag in the other. They wouldn't have left without me . . . would they? Could Bill have possibly been that determined to leave on time?

"Obelix! Obelix!"

My heart jumped. The familiar shout, now mixed with broken sentences of unfamiliar rapid French, came from the splendid monstrosity towering on the one side above me. Xavier's worried face looked down, a mix of anger and distress. He said something with finality into the mobile phone he'd been yelling into and shoved it into his pocket. He leaned over to me from high above.

"My dog is lost and this idiot has missed his plane."

That was nothing, I thought.

"Have you seen Obelix?" he asked before noticing the empty slip before me. "Where is your boat?"

I shook my head, not taking my eyes away from his. A wall of tears threatened to break if I did. He stared at me for a moment before he realized that I didn't know.

"Oh . . . "

He invited me to come on board. He took my wet towel bundle and reached for my hand to help me up. Grabbing his outstretched hand made it more difficult to climb the ladder, but I was willing to make the extra effort in exchange for experiencing what turned out to be a very solid grip.

I followed him along the deck of the boat to the spacious cockpit in the stern. I had no idea what to expect from the interior of the luxurious yacht. There had been no way to have a peek inside with the boat docked bow-first to the slip. Most of the boats in the marina were docked the other way around to allow for easier access at the stern. Not the Frenchman—he had chosen privacy over ease.

A stylish (of course) lounge area took up much of the cockpit space. I threw myself down on a curved cream-coloured bench, defeated. Xavier handed me back my shower stuff. I was really, really glad my dirty underwear hadn't fallen out. He got on the cockpit's VHF to call my uncle while I sat useless and fought back tears.

"What is the name of the boat?"

"*Quixotic.*"

There was no immediate response over the radio. He called to my uncle's boat repeatedly over the next hour, making small talk between attempts, but with no better success. He finally gave up.

He sat down across from me, his hands resting on his knees. He looked at me with genuine concern and sighed.

"At least I've still got my toothbrush," I sniffed, trying to lighten the mood. I attempted a smile.

He smiled back but it was with such pity that it didn't help at all.

"Where are they headed?" He asked.

"Across. We're . . . They're… going to Antigua."

"Ah, it is pretty there. Me, I am going to Martinique. At least, I am going there when my crew arrives. He has missed his plane, he has just told me on my mobile. He is my friend so I will forgive him. But I wanted very much to leave today."

He paused, his slender fingers drumming on his thighs in thought. His reference to his crew dashed my assumption that he was babysitting someone else's expensive yacht. He brightened as his mind grabbed hold of a plan.

"You know how to sail, yes?"

"Somewhat."

9

"Do you want to leave today?"

"Well, I did… with my family, but… You're not suggesting I sail with you instead?"

He shrugged, like it seemed a reasonable suggestion to him.

"No, I can't do that," I continued, trying to be sensitive to his desire to help, but a little surprised at the audacity of the suggestion. "I can't go anywhere before I reach Bill and Margaret—they've got my passport, my wallet. My clothes! Everything . . . "

"Except your toothbrush."

This time he really smiled, and it must have been a magical smile because it completely lifted my spirits.

"Then we will catch up to them," shrugged the Frenchman, trying to suppress a grin, "because I have a big boat."

It was going to be hard to turn him down.

He led me on a tour of the inside of his yacht, *Orion*. I thought I'd walked onto a classic vintage James Bond set. Her look was sleek and gorgeous—for 1965. The marine architecture was beautifully manifested: walnut sliding panels, a multitude of hidden compartments, and compact built-in furniture. The overall effect was style, but Style with a capital S for *Show-off.* Everything that wasn't finished with walnut was either cream-coloured leather or gold.

The first room in the cabin, down a few steps from the cockpit area, was a small lounge with built-in seats. The seats curved slightly at every corner of their cream and gold cushions, nested within the walls of panelled walnut. The seats were low and deep, proportionally very square. On one side a tall walnut slab rose to the ceiling. Its gold lines hinted at lounge-type goodies hidden within. The ceiling itself was divided up into cream cloth rectangles, separated by gold coloured reveals. The lines at the centre framed a solid skylight, through which the boom was clearly visible. Elegantly framed porthole windows, also in gold, ran along both port and starboard walls. At the end of the lounge the walnut backs of the seats came forward into two low walls, between which a set of steps went further down into a space-age navigational area.

An instrument-rich panel cradled a star-trek chair on the

starboard side of the nav-station. The VHS and SSB radios, the GPS, the radar, the electronics, and so on were controlled from here. Opposite the control booth, on the port side, a fold-down table was laid out with maps of the Atlantic, and charts of the local Canary Islands. The smart walnut cabinets above hinted at more maps, books, and charts. The whole station continued the theme of fine gold reveals and smooth wood panels. A gold-coloured rail wrapped itself around the space at the end, flowing down another set of steps which followed the curved shape of the nav-station floor.

The steps led into the main saloon, a large area consisting of a dining space, a galley kitchen, and more bench seating. A hallway led behind the nav-station to the area under the cockpit, but Xavier didn't include that in the tour. I followed him into the saloon instead. The dining area snuggled against the curved edge of the nav-station, reflecting its shape where the seats wrapped around a circular dining table, much like the lounge seating in the cockpit outside. The dining area opened on a thoroughly modern galley kitchen equipped with a gimballed stainless-steel gas stove, a stainless-steel fridge hidden beneath the counter, and translucent Plexiglas cupboards hiding everything else. At the end of the kitchen a second small hallway cradled three wooden doors. One was the yacht's head. The others led to the two V-berth cabins.

"You can have this one, if you like," said the Frenchman, referring to the larger of the two. I found the offer presumptuous, given my declining his invitation to join him.

"Uh, I'm not sure this is a good idea," I managed. On the other hand I had nowhere else to go.

He responded by stepping across the threshold into the six by eight foot space and putting his hand against another walnut-panelled surface. He pushed in and slid the panel sideways to reveal a series of shallow shelves inside. He was excited by the closet, as if it were part of a favourite toy. He beckoned me to have a look. I squeezed into the tiny space with him, aware the close proximity might breach the shell I had built around myself. When I felt my arm brush against his bare skin, the soft touch sent a warm flush up my neck and across my face. I shifted away before he noticed.

"I don't think I'll need that," I said, indicating the small towel bundle in my hand. The gesture gave away the slim chance that I might consider taking him up on his offer. My conflicted sentiments confused me. On the one hand I was curious about him and his obviously very comfortable yacht. On the other hand, to sail away with a complete stranger was absolute idiocy.

"It was a suggestion only…" he said, somewhat deflated.

"I know nothing about you," I replied, looking around at the over-the-top interior of the yacht. "And what about you? You don't even know my name."

"Then it is not a problem with the shelf…"

"No, the shelf is not the problem." I would have laughed if I wasn't so exasperated.

"I understand," he nodded. "You do not know that you can trust me. Me, I think it is a great idea to sail with you and catch up to your family. I need a second person to sail, and we could help each other. But I know me. Perhaps if you spoke to someone who also knows me?"

He convinced himself that was the solution, and beckoned me to follow him outside, searching through the speed dial of his cell on the way back through *Orion*'s cabin. He found the number he was looking for and called it as we arrived back at the cockpit lounge. He handed me the phone.

"It is dialling my record label," was all he said.

His record label? Was he a French musician with the aesthetic taste of an Arab Sheik?

A woman answered in French, identifying the company with a name so abstract that it could have represented anything from a record company to a curb-side lottery shack. Between my broken French and her fast Parisian accent, our conversation was very confused. I eventually resolved to my satisfaction that the man I was being tempted to entrust my safety to was a good man. She clarified that when he referred to "my record label" he meant it literally—he owned it. She was also clear that I was pretty damn lucky to be with him. He laughed hard as the conversation unfolded.

His laughter reminded me that only days ago any sort of humour had been out of reach. My life had held no value to me. I had barely taken the risk of inhaling. Why did I hold it in such esteem now? This sailing trip I had embarked on represented a big step in grabbing a hold of life again. Here dangled an even bigger carrot. I couldn't resist his laughter. I swallowed the fear and succumbed to the urge to take a bolder, more dangerous bite.

I held out my hand to him in proper introduction and committed to sailing with him.

"Now if only I can find my dog," said Xavier.

***

Xavier leant me a wad of Euros to replace my lost sun hat before we left, and anything else I felt I couldn't do without. I managed to get myself a hat, a couple of t-shirts, and a sarong. Anything else I would have to borrow from him.

He left all his contact information with the harbour master in case Bill and Margaret got in touch before we reached them ourselves. On our way back from the marina office a freshly groomed Obelix yapped at us from the cockpit of a nearby yacht.

"Obelix, c'est toi?" laughed Xavier in disbelief. "Qu'est-ce que tu fais ici?"

A pudgy middle-aged woman wearing a loose t-shirt emblazed with "It's better in Bonaire" and accompanying close-fitting lime green shorts appeared from the galley below. Obelix ran to her, his entire back half wagging with his tail. The dog danced a jig between us, a big grin on his face.

"Is he yours?" The woman asked, worry hanging off her question. She added, with a combined defensive-accusatory tone, "We found him wandering by himself last night. He seemed hungry."

"He likes you, I think," observed Xavier. My sexy companion admitted at this point that he'd only found Obelix two weeks before, and worried about taking a stray dog on his next sail. I marvelled at how Xavier phrased his words so that the cruiser would take his dog and feel like she was doing him a favour.

We returned to *Orion*, leaving Obelix behind in exuberant hands.

"He will be ok, yes?" Xavier paused behind me, half way up the ladder to the deck. Hurt spread across his gorgeous face as the truth sank in that he would not see his dog again.

"He'll be fine. In the six hours she had him she's already given him a haircut," I smiled.

"That is why I am worried," said Xavier, his eyes brightening.

"And what about me?" I asked as he stepped into the cockpit. We had nothing left on our agenda but imminent departure.

"You would like a haircut?"

"No. Am I going to be ok? With you?" My question deflated his joke.

"I promise," he said. He held his hand out to shake mine, all humour in his eyes replaced by solemn sincerity. "I promise that you will be safe and that you will arrive with your uncle and your aunt very soon. I will make sure this happens."

I accepted his handshake, with the sense that he meant his promise, but also that I was probably just another homeless stray to him. As my hand lingered in the strong warmth of his, I decided to accept that role. We would only be together for a few days, anyway.

We unleashed ourselves from the dock.

***

Xavier motored slowly out of the Puerto de Mogan harbour and for another hour out to sea before we put up the sails and cut the engine. The winds were unsteady, but good enough for Xavier to guide me through *Orion*'s sailing specifics. The boat was rigged with a large main sail and three huge fore-sails all connected to a series of winches along the front edges of the cockpit. Due to the size of the yacht, and the small number of people he usually had with him, Xavier had mechanized a lot of it. The automatic furling and winches made the yacht much easier to sail than I thought it would be. This was a good thing because at night we would be taking turns sailing *Orion* alone.

We radioed Bill and Margaret every hour or so, and by the third try finally got a response. They were on their way back to Gran Canaria after discovering that I hadn't actually shut myself up in my cabin. Apparently there had been a nasty one-sided argument through the closed aft-cabin door before they had bothered to see if I was in there. They were, of course, horrified when they discovered I wasn't, and had immediately turned the boat around.

Quixotic was still a four hour sail ahead of us in shifting winds. Bill didn't want to head all the way back to Gran Canaria if it wasn't necessary. Xavier repeated his initial idea that *Orion* simply catch up to *Quixotic* in the open waters. My uncle balked. He suggested instead that we all meet in Mindelo, a small town in the Cape Verde Islands about 600 km south of us. That way we could all refuel after this nonsense and I could rejoin my correct boat safely. Xavier put up a convincing argument that Mindelo was several days out from his intended route and that if he did not divert he would have no need to refuel. I reminded Xavier that with the extra travel time involved his friend Jacques could book a new flight to join us in Cape Verde. Xavier did admit to feeling responsible for reuniting me with my family as promised, and finally acquiesced. After further and less heated discussion involving news that a late season Atlantic hurricane swelled towards the Canaries, Xavier concurred that the diversion might prove the better route after all. We promised to maintain regular contact with Bill and Margaret in the meantime.

I was transfixed watching Xavier track up and down the length of the yacht to ensure everything was in order. He double-checked lines, coiled ropes, tightened knots. His movement was almost cat-like—he never wavered or faltered. I asked him if I could help but he insisted I make myself at home in the lounge.

He offered some Dramamine, but I didn't need it. I did not feel queasy despite the constant pitching of the boat. I found the motion soothing, if anything.

He paused his work as the sun reached its zenith and

excused himself to duck inside and settle in at the navigation stool. He flicked on the SSB radio which filled the cabin air with the static of far-away French-speaking sailors. He jumped in on occasion with the same animation he had shown while speaking on his cell phone. His laughter pealed through the cabin. The anonymous speakers on the other end of the radio joined in.

He explained afterwards that the French cruising community connected over a regular radio network at the same time every day in order to share stories or information about sailing conditions. It seemed that many sailors were predicting better wind in the next day or two. Xavier concluded his explanation with an offer of fresh bread and cheeses for lunch, followed by a promise of fresh fruit. His timing was perfect.

We lounged in *Orion*'s cockpit after we ate, enjoying the sail and the sun. Xavier stretched out on the bench seat behind the wheel, keeping an eye on the boat's autopilot. I relaxed on a nearby curved lounge seat in my new outfit, wearing a pair of his sunglasses. We blasted the stereo across the water as we rolled over it. He had a great cd collection and thousands more songs on his i-pod. I pretended that the clouds of passing flying fish were jumping to the beat of his French hip hop.

He asked me about where I was from, and all the things that had happened before I'd found myself stranded at the side of a dock off the African coast. I couldn't imagine confiding to him that three days before I had been stranded on the floor of my apartment. So I skipped that ugly part, mostly. I painted a broad picture of my Canadian life, and concluded by admitting I'd had a difficult year after a bad break-up. The subject was uncomfortable for both of us, although I couldn't say what unnerved him. There was a subtle shift in our dynamic when I admitted that I was single. I didn't know his situation, but my lack of any attachment exposed possibilities that had previously remained undefined. I changed the subject and asked about him.

I learned that while he did live in Paris, he was actually Swiss, and half-Spanish on his mother's side. His parents had split when he was young, and his mother had taken him and his younger brother to live in France. He had caught the sailing bug as a kid

16

when spending summers back with his dad on Lake Geneva. Those were times he had made friends with lots of future Swiss bankers. He wasn't one of them, but instead had managed to make some decent money with a small (couldn't have been that small) electronic music label he had developed with the help of their business advice. The label earned him enough to keep the boat maintained—a boat which he had won in a vicious poker game in Vienna, and for which he'd put up one of his kidneys. The original owner had been a drug dealer based in Zanzibar who'd had a bit of a Goldfinger fixation. Hence the early James Bond interior design. I couldn't glean from Xavier how he'd ended up in a high-stakes poker game with the guy, but I guess sometimes these things just happen.

I didn't fail to notice he hadn't mentioned a girlfriend. He skirted the intimate details of his personal life masterfully. It was quite possible there were many women. It wasn't hard to imagine them lining up for the opportunity.

We determined quickly that we were both more comfortable talking about music, or Paris, or anything, other than ourselves. And that we should stick to talking about those things in English.

The wind continued to misbehave and we didn't move very fast. Six hours out and we could still faintly see the buildings of Puerto de Mogan. In the waning light of magic hour I saw a dark fin cutting through a nearby wave. Dolphins!

The pod was small, maybe 18 dolphins in total. They swam along the side of the boat, rolling through the wake in turns. I leaned over the low gold rail at the back of the cockpit to get a better look. Two of them turned on one side to look up at me, each staring from one eye. They were so close that if I just reached my hand out…

Xavier's wide hand touched my bare shoulder.

"Do not fall out of my boat, s'il vous plait," he begged. "Please."

His concern was genuine, although I had sensed no danger. The moment I sat back he removed his hand. The warmth of it remained for a brief moment before vanishing in the breeze. His touch had felt so natural. I looked at him to see if I was imagining some easy connection. His focus was on the sailing console. I turned back to the dolphins, but they had disappeared into the waves.

Before dinner we checked the weather forecast at the space-age nav-station. A laptop computer was set up to receive email via short-wave, just like on my uncle's boat. Xavier subscribed to a weather service that emailed current data files. The data plugged directly into maps of *Orion*'s position, appearing as wind direction and speed. It looked like a bunch of non-descript arrows to me, but Xavier seemed happy about the forecast. He offered me some wine to toast the better wind.

"Sure, thank you," I said. "But no getting me drunk."

"I would not do that," he frowned. He seemed genuinely insulted.

"Ok, just a little drunk then," I teased.

"No, not even a little bit," he shook his head, but his eyes were twinkling.

Xavier went below and reappeared with a bottle, plastic glasses, and two plates of food. I eyed the plates filled with marinated artichokes, dates with candied almond centres, real French brie, champagne crackers, and stuffed peppers. He said he had shelves and shelves of this stuff. It was all delicious.

Xavier offered to play a mix of his label's best artists, and the evening air was soon filled with some great electronica—some kind of afro-beat fusion, St. Germaine-influenced groups, more versions of French rap and hip hop—all of it incredibly cool.

I had enough wine in me to feel free to move about the cockpit in a marine version of dancing. Xavier joined me. He was a good dancer. We learned to make the boat's motion work for our dance moves. Or maybe he had done this before. I had not, as there had never been dancing on Bill's boat—so when a particularly large wave shoved the boat abruptly sideways, I completely lost my balance. Xavier caught me easily. I giggled until I realized we were poised to kiss.

"You are a little bit drunk, I think," observed Xavier, and put me back on my feet without following through. So I wasn't the only one caught off guard. I couldn't help wishing he was a little bit more drunk. But someone had to be responsible for sailing this 60ft James Bond movie set. We danced until the darkness enveloped us. This time he let me hold his hand for balance. He was surprisingly strong.

We had decided to split the night's sail into three alternating watches of three hours each, plus a short watch of about an hour tacked on at the end. Xavier would take the first and last of the big three hour chunks, saying that he only liked going to sleep once, and didn't need much of it. That seemed unfairly skewed to my advantage, but I didn't argue. He had to lend me some rain gear and had an auto-inflatable life-jacket with harness for me to wear. The rain gear was huge on me, and he had a hard time keeping a straight face as I tried to roll up the sleeves and the pants so as to not be swimming in them. The harness at least was adjustable. I went to get some sleep in the tiny v-berth cabin while I could.

Xavier woke me up with a quiet nudge three hours later. He had made me tea and left out more crackers and brie. He sat with me for a while before going below to get some sleep, wanting to be sure I felt comfortable with the set of the sails and the way the boat handled. When I assured him I was alright, he studied my face for a long time. The corners of his sensual lips turned up and he got up to go. He leaned over and kissed my cheek before disappearing below. He smelled like the sea.

***

Being alone in the cockpit was unnerving, despite my assurances to the contrary. I sipped my tea while my eyes adjusted, my ears embracing the sound of the waves cresting just behind the boat. The dark water slowly separated itself from the dark sky. The stars were out and falling occasionally, but the beautiful night sky was without a moon. The reflections of the brighter stars glowed on the surface of the waves. Phosphorescence in the water added its own sparkle as the boat cut through it or as nearby waves crested. Every so often a big wave would slap the boat sideways.

More often a wall of black would rise from the rear, and just as it seemed to overtake us would lift the boat to the sky and pass beneath.

I had to stand up to look around the horizon every so often, moving through the cockpit for an unobstructed view in each direction and confirming that any passing freighters didn't hit the yacht. My movement was restricted by the line that connected my harness to a metal clasp at the base of the ship's console, but that line was my only insurance against being swept overboard.

Usually some kind of vocal chatter could be heard coming over the console's radio handset when there was a ship nearby. If a freighter appeared on the horizon, most often it would pass far in the distance. Sometimes a rising star would look like a distant ship. Typically if a freighter captain felt that a sailboat was in the way, they might radio ahead to tell the smaller boat to move. It was a leap of faith to wait for a message from an approaching freighter, however. There had been occasions when a freighter had ploughed through a sleeping yacht at sea, drowning all on board.

Most of the radio chatter came from nearby fishing vessels. The voices became entertaining after awhile. Most were in Spanish and I couldn't really understand anything but the mood. I heard a few short French conversations—once I followed a conversation to the radio channel the speakers diverted to, and vaguely grasped that one of them thought a lot about Jennifer Aniston while the other was appalled, because compared to Audrey Tautou. . . I switched back.

Sometimes there was radio chatter when no boats were around. There was someone out there who would get on the radio and whistle a clear crisp note but say nothing.

After about two hours of mixed vocal entertainment, followed by a long silence peppered with shooting stars, a single English-speaking voice cut in.

"Jeremy, Jeremy . . . Jeremy, if you're out there, go to 57"
I switched to channel 57 to eavesdrop on the conversation.
" . . . never to call over the VHF."
"I've intercepted –"
"You haven't done shit, jackass."

"No one's listening."

"Wouldn't matter anyway, mate. You're done for."

A slight pause was interrupted by a whimpering strangled sound, made unclear by radio static. The hair stood up on the back of my neck.

The static increased on the channel, and I could hear a furious voice coming through, just couldn't make out any specific words except the occasional "fuck."

Then silence.

And I still had an hour to go. By myself.

Chapter 3

Venus glowed brightly enough in the sky to leave a river of light over the water, a soft pale version of the sun's or the moon's. The silhouetted fin of a black dolphin sliced the ribbon in two.

My thrill at seeing another dolphin pushed the eerie radio conversation from my thoughts, and caused me to forget Xavier's fear of my leaning out over the water. The dolphin appeared next to the boat, swimming sideways to look up at me with a grin. It disappeared as suddenly as it had arrived, leaving black lapping water in its wake.

I felt a hand on my shoulder.

I jumped, but it was just Xavier. He laughed his endearing laugh that verged on a giggle.

I told him about the weird VHF conversation. He raised his eyebrows, but pointed out that it was hard to know what was really going on with a few disconnected sentences. He added that his radio was set to pick up signals from far away, so even if strange events had occurred, they could have happened anywhere. Whatever had or hadn't happened out there, there was nothing we could do about it at the moment. He was right, and his reality check gave me some comfort. So did his long warm embrace.

"I wanted to kiss you earlier," He confessed as he broke away.

"What stopped you?" My heart was racing.

"I think that your uncle would like that I deliver you safely."

"You mean it's not safe to kiss you?" I teased.

"I don't know," he chuckled. "But I respect your uncle. I

would not like him to think that I took advantage."

"Hey, I decide who takes advantage of me."

He shrugged through his fatigue.

I kissed him instead, to make my point; a simple kiss, quick but well-placed. I pulled away just as his soft lips accepted mine and started to part. I felt my face flush immediately at my own boldness. I turned away and crawled off to sleep in the bow before it went any further. Xavier didn't stop me.

***

I awoke gasping from a nasty dream to find myself in the quiet fore cabin with the fancy shelves. I heard only the sound of water rushing along the sides of the hull, felt the rocking motion of the boat in the waves push and pull on my body. I'd fallen asleep wearing the rain gear, but checking my borrowed clock I could see that it was already time for my second, shorter watch anyway. I made my way through the dark salon, holding myself steady against various solid objects as I passed them. I found Xavier lying on one of the cockpit benches, staring up at the stars. A pair of headphones leaked a tinkling facsimile of whatever he was listening to. He smiled when he saw me out of the corner of his eye, a slight twitch in which belied his exhaustion. He made no mention of my earlier kiss. Instead, he insisted I take his i-pod for my watch. I didn't argue.

With music, the night became magic. There was a certain comfort in blocking out the sound of the cresting waves breaking nearby, not to mention the obliteration of any wayward VHF traffic. The sweet melodies brightened the stars, made the phosphorescence more prolific. The motion of the waves, both up and down and back and forth, always somehow coincided with the rhythm of the music, and it felt like dancing in space. The sensation turned me on with a rush I hadn't felt for a long, long time.

***

The next day Xavier decided he should go over the boat more thoroughly with me, in case something happened to him. I hesitated—even if it was true that I wouldn't be able to sail *Orion* on my own, we were only sailing together for a few days. However he insisted that I learn and we spent the morning changing tacks until I understood how the mechanized winches worked. We took only one quick break for his regularly scheduled French radio net, at which point he took advantage of the opportunity to show me how to use the SSB.

Palpable electricity hung in the air all morning. The extra charge hadn't existed the day before—not even the night before. Or was I imagining it? His touch sang when our skin brushed together. His grip lingered when he reached out to help me balance across the deck. Had he changed his mind? It was driving me crazy.

Sometimes I felt Xavier's eyes on me as we worked the sails together. He'd look away when I returned his gaze, like I wasn't supposed to catch him staring. It felt like he was trying to make a decision, and was examining me for clues. I'd made my own decision the moment I found myself a breath away from his lips. I was ready for anything with him.

By noon I had memorized all the lines for the big sails. We had furled in the big genoa and let out the smaller stay sail, then put the genoa back up. We had reefed in the main, then reefed it in further, then raised it back to its full height. Just as I was thinking I wasn't having fun anymore, we found ourselves working out the optimum tack and sail positions in perfect agreement. We settled on a course that had *Orion* slicing through the waves ahead of us.

After a well-deserved lunch I felt like I needed a shower. Xavier showed me how the tricky plumbing worked, and I bathed quickly before my afternoon lesson on *Orion*'s navigation instruments. I climbed back up to the cockpit to dry off in the sun. Xavier rested at the wheel, arms stretched out on the back of the bench to either side, legs out straddling the console. He'd taken his shirt off and laid it beside himself on the seat. His head leaned back back, face soaking up the sun, eyes closed behind his sunglasses. I could see his muscles moving subtly to counterbalance the movement of the boat. He opened one eye and looked at me without moving his head. He beckoned with a finger.

"I need to teach you more," he said.

"How are you going to teach me when that's all the energy you have?" I teased.

He reached out when I got close and pulled me down to sit beside him at the console. He managed to tuck his arm around my waist in the process.

"The beauty of *Orion*," he replied, "is that she does not require very much work."

He walked me through all the electronics and made sure I knew how to do everything at least once with no errors. He toured me through the autopilot and the console chart plotter. I learned how to turn the engine on and off. I even radioed my uncle's boat but they were too far away to hear the signal. Finally it appeared that Xavier felt satisfied I could handle the boat if necessary. He asked how well I knew my sailing knots. I groaned.

"Knot very well," I said, but the bad pun was lost in translation.

We discovered that there was a gap in the names we had for many of the different knots we knew, a result of the French and British being at war so often during the height of naval power.

Xavier questioned me about the 'clove hitch', which sounded funny to him. I looked around for something to demonstrate with. He grabbed a loose line from a bin below one of the seats and handed it to me. He held out his bare forearm for me to tie the knot around. I was distracted for a moment, the rich colour of his tanned skin accentuating the strong muscles underneath as he held his hand in a fist. He did not fail to notice. He laughed and teased me that I hesitated because I didn't know the knot.

Then it was his turn, and I held out my arm so he could demonstrate a "noeud plat." I watched his graceful fingers deftly tie a reef knot. We took turns back and forth, playing with different knots. There was an odd intimacy to it—like playing a kind of children's "trust" game. Eventually we ran out of knots.

"I am thinking," mused Xavier while toying with the loose

line, "that you will not know the pirate knot."

"The pirate knot? Is that supposed to be the English or the French name?"

He gestured for my arm, without answering my question. He wore a very serious expression, yet there was that little turn at the corners of his sexy mouth like he was hiding a secret joke. He tied a loose knot around my wrist, similar to a slip knot but with an extra loop. Then he indicated he needed my other hand as well.

I shot him a wary look but presented my free hand to meet his challenge. He guided my hand through the extra loop, then pulled the loop snug until I found myself with my wrists tied together, my hands facing each other, and Xavier holding a long end leading from them. I stared at the results, frowning.

"The pirate knot," he explained in mock triumph, "is for when you are attacked by pirates, and you need to make them your prisoner after you have overcome them. The knot cannot be undone except by me."

"Let me guess—a Lake Geneva invention?"

"Close, but no. Chamonix. I was twelve years."

"I've been to Chamonix. I think I was also 12 . . . "

"Oh . . . then you know the pirate knot?"

But he knew very well that I did not.

I glanced up from my imprisoned wrists to find him deep in study of my reaction to this unexpected turn of events. Xavier said nothing, but his eyes—their blue-violet so deep I could fall into them—were expecting something from me. I was too nervous to know what response he was hoping for, or needing to see. I was also a little annoyed.

"Are you going to teach me how to tie it then?" I asked.

"No. It is my secret knot," he laughed.

He pulled the line closer so that my hands rested across his lap and I was leaning into him. I could feel his grip against my fingertips. I hadn't taken my eyes off his, and he held my gaze. His free hand reached up to caress my cheek before he leaned in and kissed me on the lips. It was a deep and sensual kiss I hadn't really expected. I returned it fully as his hand slipped around to the back of my neck to hold me. Our tongues pushed together for a tentative taste.

Xavier pulled away with difficulty and stood up at the console with his back to me. The hand holding the line to my wrists trailed behind him, but he did not let go of it. I watched him inspect the sails, our course plot, and the horizon, my annoyance fading as my anticipation grew. I hadn't had sex in so long. Was I ready? Like swimming, sometimes it was better to dive headfirst into the deep end—if that's what was going on here. I wasn't completely sure. When he seemed satisfied with the autopilot, he turned back to me, but made no move to free my hands.

"Aren't you going to untie me?" I asked.

"If you prefer… But in my practice, one must always ravage pirates before letting them go."

"Don't you mean 'ravish'?" I whispered.

"Then, I must 'ravish' you?"

"Um… yes, please," I begged.

He grinned and lifted me over his shoulder like I weighed nothing. I screamed with delight. He gripped my legs with one hand and caressed my ass with the other. He was turning me on, but I pretended to object, making feeble attempts to hit his back while I hung upside-down. We left the brightness of the cockpit and caroused our way through Orion's cabin. When we wound down the nav station stairs, Xavier turned right, into the room he'd kept from me earlier. This would be the state room, I guessed—the master suite of the Goldfinger yacht. But the only thing I could see for the moment was Xavier's muscular brown back.

He swung me off his shoulder and on to the bed. I bounced as he climbed on with me, kneeling on either side of my legs. He pulled the long end of the cord through a loop at the base of the headboard, all the way through so that my hands fit tight against the flat surface, my arms above my head. He tied the loose end to a porthole latch high up on the wall where I couldn't reach it, then sat back on my legs and looked at me. He gauged my reaction closely.

Above him, I could see myself floating on the ceiling.

"There's a mirror above your bed," I said, distracted.

"Goldfinger," mused Xavier, smiling. "He said he never

slept with less than 8 women at a time."

"And you?"

"I try to limit myself to three or four."

He drank me in with his dark blue eyes, laughing when I didn't appreciate his joke. My legs brushed back and forth against his as the boat rocked us, teasing like it was coaxing us to play. Xavier's laughter was infectious.

"Well, there's only one of me," I smiled. I added, "And I'm not a pirate."

"But somehow," he laughed, "you have managed to commandeer my ship and have me chasing strangers across the sea."

He straightened my t-shirt absently as we both reflected on the truth of this.

"That was your idea," I remembered. But Xavier's thoughts had moved on to other things.

His hand lingered on my breast a moment, his thumb casually circling in search of a nipple under the fabric. I shifted beneath him when he found one, then the other. He responded by planting a lingering kiss on my mouth. I closed my eyes and welcomed his soft lips. His tongue pushed in for a taste of mine before his kisses moved to my neck, where his breath heated my skin. I looked up and watched the rippling reflection above me of his other hand slipping under my shirt. His warm palm slid up along my belly and inside the top of my bikini. He squeezed my breast hard, murmuring in my ear how soft I was. I pulled at the rope holding my hands against the headboard as warmth flooded through me.

He felt me strain and sat up for a moment to check on me. My heart was pounding hard and fast.

"Don't stop," I urged. The corners of his mouth twitched up.

"Pirate," he accused, grinning at me.

He hooked his thumbs under the hem of my t-shirt, and peeled it up over my head—but not quite the whole way. He left the t-shirt covering my eyes, the rest of it further binding my arms above my head. I felt his mouth on mine as he kissed me hard, and

I understood he planned to leave me blindfolded that way. I succumbed to the heightened sensation of his touch.

He pulled away, but I couldn't see what he was doing now. His thumb slowly traced my open lips. I licked it, and closed my mouth around it while he caressed my cheek with his fingers. Then the hand was gone.

Now both his hands were at my bikini top, pulling the fabric down to expose my breasts. He squeezed them while I felt his breath at my neck, his bristly cheek rough against mine. His hands slipped under me, lifting me slightly to undo my bikini. He pulled the top up over my head, lingering to kiss me on the mouth while he was there.

"Commandeered my ship . . . naughty pirate," he whispered hotly in my ear.

"I'll... get you back... for this," I managed.

"I can't wait," he laughed.

He licked and sucked his way southwards until his wet tongue arrived at a nipple. I groaned with pleasure as I felt his lips wrap around it, his tongue toying with me.

I tried to squirm but was restricted by the clothes around my arms and by his weight straddling my legs. He slid his hands down to my waist, following them with continuous slow, hot-breathed kisses. He stopped and sat up.

I was conscious of how heavy I was breathing, knowing he was watching me closely. My stomach clenched in unsure anticipation of whatever pleasurable sensation was coming next. He shifted his weight, the muscles of his calves straining against my bare thighs.

"Do your worst," I challenged blindly, unsure if I knew what I was asking for.

I heard an amused grunt, and felt his warmth again as he leaned in to focus on my other nipple. The tip of his wet tongue teased the nub before his entire mouth engulfed it, hot and sucking. He nibbled with his teeth which sent a combined jolt of pleasure and pain shooting straight to my groin.

"Oh, God!" I gasped, my hips arching up towards him in response. He murmured back, but his mouth was full. His hands squeezed my hips as he coaxed them back down. The muscles in his legs tightened. His breath grew heavy and fast.

He bit me again.

I moaned sharply. The metal loop the rope was tied to clanked as I jerked against it.

Xavier licked a path of hot kisses down my exposed skin until he reached the waistband of my shorts. He sat up to undo the clasp. I felt the cool air seep in against the warmth and wetness inside when he drew the zipper down. My legs tensed up beneath him and he paused to caress my thigh. He muttered something in French that I didn't quite catch, but the tone was full of wonder and affection. His weight shifted off the bed entirely. I missed his touch, and burned with hunger for more. His fingers brushed along the skin of my waist and slipped inside both my shorts and my bikini bottoms as he grasped the edges of the waistbands. He pulled them off together in one smooth motion. I heard them land somewhere on the floor at the end of the bed.

I was now completely naked.

I heard him undo his own shorts and step out of them. I craned my head back to try to see under the edge of my shirt blindfold.

"Are you peeking?" he mocked.

"I want to know what you look like," I complained in the general direction of his voice.

"I am very good looking. And as you have seen I have a very large ship."

"Yes, but men are known to use large vehicles to compensate for lack of size elsewhere," I teased. I reached my foot out towards the sound of his voice, hoping to touch him.

He grasped my searching ankle with a strong hand.

"You will have to wait to find out," he informed me, and pulled my foot up toward him. The motion stretched me tight against the rope around my wrists. I cried out in surprise until my toes were engulfed by the overwhelming wet warmth of his mouth. He kissed and suckled each toe until the heat crawled up my legs to my core and I purred like a kitten.

He laid my leg back down beside the other.

His firm hands slipped between my knees and pushed my legs apart. His silky skin brushed against the inside of my thighs as he crawled between them, sending my heart racing. I was a trembling bowl of jelly. I yearned for whatever was coming.

Xavier caressed the insides of my thighs softly, murmuring to me in French. I moved my hips towards him but he guided them back. He adjusted his body between my legs so that he gripped my thighs against his strong shoulders. His soft hair bristled against the inside of my legs, preceding the heat of his breath as he moved in. The warmth of a tender kiss against my clit aroused me further. I caressed his back with my feet until he slipped his hot tongue into my crack and drew a long wet line upwards. I lost any control I had left of my body. I gasped and squirmed against his grip as the tip of his tongue played mercilessly at my screaming clit. He wrapped his mouth around it and began to suck, sending a wave of torrential pleasure shooting out in all directions. My toes curled against the silky skin of his back, scratching him. My fingers grabbed in vain at the wooden headboard above me. The wave echoed back to my hips and shattered in a convulsive tremor at my stomach.

As my body softened, Xavier warned, "We are not finished."

"I know," I gasped.

My knees still rested across his shoulders. He leaned forward and braced himself on the bed, forcing my hips up and my legs apart. I could feel the hot tip of his cock flirting at the wet opening between my legs, nudging my clit and teasing me. My hips, with a life of their own, chased him, needing to swallow him now. I'd feel the heat of him pause to slide in for a moment, then move away.

"Xavier!" I admonished as he teased the entrance with only an inch of himself.

He complied, pushing in deep until I could feel him all the way at the end. He thrust again right away, but held himself against me, the pressure of his pelvic bone against mine creating a garden of Nirvana through my whole body, making me tremble. He waited there as wave after wave rolled through me. I cried out. He let one of my legs slip off his shoulder so he could reach up to push the t-shirt off my eyes. I blinked at the return of daylight before meeting his delighted gaze. He kissed me hungrily, moaning between heavy breathes, and then returned to fucking me. The knee still held in place by his bent arm was practically against my chest, keeping me wide open to his thrusts. He drove in fast, then began to slow. His gaze fixed on mine, judging my momentum, smiling coyly as my obvious ecstasy increased. He sped up as I was coming again, driving harder and harder towards his own climax until the final enveloping waves shuddered through both of us and he collapsed against me with a smiling sigh.

My other leg fell from across his shoulder. He rolled over beside me, letting cool air creep across our bodies. He slid his hands beneath me to the small of my back and let his head fall against my chest. He was breathing hard, sweating and trying to catch his breath.

"Merde," he said, laughing. He turned his head and kissed my upturned arm. He reached above me and untied the line that held my arms in place. I offered my wrists with their t-shirt bundle out to him so he could undo his knot. It took seconds. I shook the bikini top and t-shirt off.

"I have to go to check on the boat," sighed Xavier, although he didn't make a move to go at first. With a second deep sigh he extricated himself from my limbs and moved to pick his shorts up off the floor. I drank in the sight of his beautiful body as he got dressed.

"I will come right back," he said as he finished tying the string around his waist. I reached for my scattered clothes and began to dress.

"I will just be a moment," interrupted Xavier, stopping me. "Unless you have had enough?"

I threw my clothes on the floor and told him to hurry.

Chapter 4

While I waited I found myself staring at my reflection in
the ceiling. My pale skin was a stark contrast to the dark brown
cover on the bed. I watched as all my soft parts rolled back and
forth across my front in syncopation with the waves outside. The
constant motion kept me horny. I pictured Xavier's bronzed arms
caressing me in the mirror, but I could hear him somewhere else on
the boat, shouting to be heard over a weak cell signal. He would be
a while. I fell asleep.

When I woke up the light in the room was dimmer. I was
still alone, which bothered me. I could hear faint kitchen noises
drifting through the open door. I decided to investigate.

I rolled off the bed and, still completely naked, made my
way out to the galley area. I almost collided with Xavier as he
rounded the corner of the tiny hallway outside the state room. He
had a plate of food piled high in one hand, and a bottle of wine in
the other. Apart from a cloth draped over one arm, the only thing
he wore was a look of excited anticipation.

His face dropped when he saw the wounded look on mine.

"You were asleep," he explained. "I didn't want to wake
you."

"You're lucky you're so hot," I retorted as I reached out
and grabbed the bottle from him. I turned and bounced back into
the state room with it, leaving him to follow behind.

The wine was loosely corked, so I helped myself to a long
swig as Xavier came in to put the plate and the cloth down on the
bed. There wasn't a lot of space in the cabin so when I tried to
avoid hitting Xavier with the bottle I accidentally spilled wine all

down my chin. He turned to see why I was giggling.

"Attention! Le vin!" He feigned alarm.

He jumped up and tried to catch the running drips with his tongue. It tickled and I collapsed in a giggling pile on the bed next to the food, pulling him on top of me.

We ate in bed and the food was more of a diversion than a dinner. He'd managed to choose food that was accompanied by different sauces. We spent more time licking sauce off each other than off the plate. Our meal culminated with him eating me like an ice cream cone, and likewise I him. We polished off the wine.

"I could do this all day with you," Xavier reflected with quiet satisfaction, almost to himself.

"I think we just did," I added, rubbing my fingers against his rough cheek to clean off a spot of rogue relish.

He took my hand in his and kissed my wrist. He sighed in agreement, then coaxed me up so that we might return to sailing his very large ship.

I found myself, hours later, back in the state room trying to fall asleep after Xavier had slipped off for his night watch. The room, situated at the more stable stern end of the yacht, was a palace compared to the small cupboard my three pieces of clothing sat in. My eyes adjusted to the dark. The mirror in the ceiling reflected what little light seeped into the room. My skin was so pale I was a white ghost floating above myself.

I could hear Xavier's muffled voice coming from the cockpit above me. He was speaking rapid French. He was much more animated when speaking his native language than when he spoke English to me. I assumed he was talking on his mobile—he spoke on his phone whenever he had the time. I was surprised he could still get a signal even though we were only a hundred or so miles off the coast of Africa. But maybe it wasn't a great signal, given that he was shouting, and saying 'pardon?' a lot. I heard him swear in exasperation and slam the phone down. Then it was quiet.

I never did get to sleep, and when Xavier came to get me for my watch I was already dressed in the raingear. He had made the offer to sit with me in the cockpit for a bit at the start of all my shifts, since the night the radio traffic had spooked me. I looked forward to those moments when our duties overlapped, and we could let our minds wander in lackadaisical conversation. Xavier had other ideas this time. He was more tired than I was, and kept the talk sweet but brisk. I invited him into some easy exchange but he was more interested in finding a pillow. I let it go.

There were no mysterious voices during either of my watches that night. The excitement emerged instead as a drop-dead gorgeous sunrise at the end. The sky lightened and glowed pink as the stars faded. The early morning hue covered the distant clouds with a candy coating. As the sun itself began to poke up on the horizon, Xavier appeared at the doorway, hair dishevelled like it was when I first met him. He rubbed his eyes and stubbly cheeks with his slender fingers. He was no longer wearing his raingear— he stood completely nude. He leaned against the doorframe with his arms crossed, sceptical about the sight of me curled up on my side along the ivory bench seat, half asleep.

Through semi-closed eyes I watched his effortless steps cross the cockpit lounge, where he tucked himself into the space at the crook of my waist.

"You're naked," I mumbled, stating the obvious.

"And you are not," he replied, playing with the voluminous fabric of my borrowed rain pants. "How's the sailing?"

I could tell he was goading me. I twisted my shoulders flat to get a better look at him.

"Everything's fine," I promised, reaching to touch his naked leg in a gesture of assurance. I knew there were no boats anywhere around us—I'd just looked.

He sat back against me, surveying the horizon. He stretched one arm out across my legs as if they were the back of the bench seat. Without looking he picked up my assuring hand with his other one and kissed it warmly.

"Aren't you hot in all this rain gear?" he challenged, his attention now on the heavy sleeve of my jacket.

"No," I said, tightening the jacket around me. It was still early and the light morning wind had a chill to it. Never mind I was too sleepy to move much. I was also self-conscious about having nothing on underneath, despite the events of the previous afternoon.

Our eyes locked in an unspoken stand-off. He still had my hand in his and, as if not to startle me with any unexpected moves, lowered it slowly to the seat. He shifted his leg to pin my hand underneath his thigh. He took advantage of my dismay as a distraction and caught me completely off guard for his follow-up move. He grabbed my free hand, which had been casually resting across my waist, and held it against the back of the seat with a firm grip while his resting arm appeared from nowhere to pull down the zipper of my rain gear.

"No!" I shouted in surprise, although I was laughing. I easily slipped my pinned hand out from under his bare leg and grabbed at his wrist to stop him from completely unzipping me. He was already half way down by the time I got a good hold and though I made the unzipping more difficult for him, his strength made my effort virtually futile. By the time he had reached the buckle near the bottom of the inflatable life-jacket, I was merely holding on to enjoy the sensation of his muscles flexing under my fingers. I didn't even notice him let go of my other hand when he needed both of his to undo the harness.

"Success!" he giggled at me, pushing back the lifejacket to get through the last of the jacket's zipper. He folded back the front of the rain gear, peeling me like the soft ripening fruit I was.

"You are naked!" He imitated me. His hand generously caressed my freshly exposed belly. He grinned at me as his hand moved to warm each breast with a gentle knead. I returned his smile, allowing him his small victory.

He relaxed against my middle, stretching his arm back out across my hips. I rested my hand back on his bare leg, enjoying the sensation of his muscles working to counterbalance the boat's constant motion.

"I must get to the business of sailing my boat," he teased with a shrug, abandoning his initiation of my arousal. I could see when he stood up that he was abandoning his own as well. He indicated the console at the end of the cockpit. "I will be over there, if you care to get up and join me."

I cursed his tight ass as he moved away from me.

I struggled upright with great difficulty, letting the jacket and harness slip off behind me. Goose bumps rose from my naked skin at the cool ocean breeze, pinching my bare nipples into upright perkiness. I knew, even though I did not look to confirm it, that he was watching my every move.

I attempted a graceful stagger to the console, bracing myself along the bench seat for balance. Xavier reached out to me with one hand when I came close enough, and pulled me into a tight embrace. The cold console wheel grazed the skin of my back, sending light shivers up my spine. I snuggled closer to Xav.

I wrapped myself around him, drawing heat against the morning breezes that caressed us from the sea. I tilted my head up and met his lips—warm, wet, and salty. We let our tongues play together in a pretense of devouring each other. I slid my hands down the hard lines of his back to the muscles of his ass and squeezed. His own hand caressed the small of my back before continuing across the dimple at the base of my spine. He paused a moment to snap the elastic waistband of the rain pants with a chuckle before sliding his hand under to curve over the arc of my bare ass beneath.

"What about those pants?" he taunted. He slipped his fingers between my legs and slid them up the middle as far as they would go.

"Stop it!" I squealed with a grin. My fingers dug into his taut butt cheeks. He eased his teasing and slid his hand out. I relaxed in the lull, fully aware of the wet heat that was left between my legs where his hand had been.

He pulled back, gazing at me with those ocean-deep eyes. He had a hard time breaking away to scan the horizon.

I turned around to face the console, snuggling my body against his. While he feigned a steady concentration on sailing, his free hand slid across my front as if to touch the largest area possible. I held his arm there, marvelling at how his tanned forearm hardened when he squeezed my breast. Another part of him was hardening, too. I reached between us, feeling for his growing erection, and ran my fingers along his smooth length when I found it. His breath sucked in sharply and he squeezed me harder, his grip becoming painful. I moaned and he let go of my breast to grab me at the waist instead. His lips parted against the nape of my neck and the warmth of his breath coursed through my blood to the growing heat between my legs. I leaned back into him, guiding the hand on my waist back up to my chilled breast. He pinched the stiffened nipple between his thumb and fingers. My stomach clenched and beneath the rain pants a line of wet threatened to run down my leg.

"Please fuck me," I panted, grabbing hold of his erection and squeezing.

"I cannot," he grimaced, the knuckles of his hand on the steering wheel glowing white in the sunlight. His hot tongue lingered in my ear.

"Put it on autopilot!" I gasped, letting my thumb trace a circle through the wetness emerging from the tip of his cock.

"It's not that," he groaned. He freed my deliciously aching nipple and clapped his hand between my legs over the rain pants. He pinched my clit between a generous bunch of material and held tight until my legs began to shake. Through shortened breath he muttered, with a grin, "I cannot fuck you in this rain gear."

"Oh my god, just take them off!" I laughed, releasing my grip on him.

He picked me up by the waist with one arm while with the other he locked our bearing with the console's computer. *Orion* could sail herself for a short while at least. I clung to his arm, shrieking through my fits of laughter, as he swung me around to face the stern.

"Hold on to the railing," he advised as our knees pressed against the edge of the bench below it, adjusting to the boat's swaying. But the railing ran along the back of the seat, requiring me to lean out towards the rolling wake and the vast ocean beyond. He tired of my hesitation and under the guidance of his gentle warm hands leaned forward with me and pressed my palms against the cold metal rail.

"Are you sure it's safe?"

"Hold on tight," he suggested—and even though I could not see his face I could hear his grin. Xavier traced hot kisses down the tingling valley between my shoulder blades. His hands slid down my arms and along my sides to tuck inside the elastic waist band of the rain pants, drawing them down to my knees. I shook the pants down the rest of the way, stepped out, and kicked them aside with one foot. Xavier tucked his toes between my bare ankles and pushed my legs out to either side of him. With his hips now up against mine I could feel the hard curve of his erection pressing against the soft moist flesh between my open legs. His hands caressed the insides of my naked thighs while his lips formed a smile against the skin of my shoulders. I moaned and arched back into him. He teased my clit with his thumb, sending my body into a shudder against him. The rest of his fingers opened me up and guided his hard cock inside me. I gasped and clutched the railing tighter as he filled me all the way. He grasped my hips, and began moving in and out in a slow rhythm. Each thrust took me a little higher, cut my breath a little shorter, and as he sped up, left my legs a little weaker. Xavier's strong hands held onto my waist firmly but when he slipped one hand forward between my legs and tickled my clit, I completely buckled. Xavier's other hand appeared like magic at the rail to brace us both. We laughed together and repositioned ourselves. Xavier resumed his thrusts—lighter but faster. He continued to play with my clit as he moved inside me. My entire body trembled as the high pressure spread from my legs up my belly through my heart and out along my limbs and finally exploded in a double fantasmic wave that came from the centre of it all. I felt him shudder with me as he pushed in deep one last time, holding himself inside until he half-collapsed against me.

"I do not think I will be able to give you back," he gasped with a soft giggle against my ear.

I turned my head to respond with a deep kiss. I didn't think I could leave, either.

We kneeled on the bench as one, our hips still locked together. His hand let go of the rail to embrace me. He slipped out at some point but we sat like that for a while, the sun warming our bodies despite the brisk sea air. Eventually he suggested I try to grab a little more sleep. I was out as soon as my head hit the pillow.

When I awoke later the boat was eerily quiet. The rushing water sounds I had become accustomed to were missing, and the boat's usual tossing was barely evident. Pale hazy light seeped in through the pill-shaped porthole windows above the bed. I grabbed my sarong and t-shirt from the end of the bed and threw them on before going back to the cockpit.

I discovered why the boat was so silent when I emerged from the cabin. The water was almost flat, and closed in by a dense fog. The sails were furled and the engine was on—so quiet I had barely heard the motor's hum. Xavier stood at the wheel, scowling. He was piloting *Orion* with assistance from the boat's radar, the chart visible on the console screen. His tension was evident when I touched his arm.

"I hate fog," he complained.

I said it reminded me of a bad movie I knew.

There was a small dot at the centre of the radar image. I asked if that was us. To my surprise he said, "No." He must not have noticed it until then because he pulled back on the throttle fast.

We slowed to less than a crawl. Both of us searched the fog for the source of the dot indicated just off our starboard bow. We heard it before we saw it—a flapping sound in the air. Through the heavy mist a lone yacht took shape. It floated in the current, its sail torn by a wide rip stemming from the centre of the mast.

There was no sign of anyone on board.

Xavier got on the VHF radio and called to the boat several times. No response. Apprehension wove its way down the back of my neck. I had not forgotten the chilling conversation I had overheard during my first watch alone. Now this.

Xavier radioed for any coast guard in the area, then got on the satellite phone to the Canary Island Coast Guard. It was the first time I'd heard him speak Spanish—he was fluent.

He handed me the wheel and directed me to circle the stranded yacht. While I steered us in a lazy arc, he dropped a number of fenders down the starboard side of the boat, and fastened a dock line to the mid cleat.

"We're going on board?" I asked doubtfully.

"I am," he said, taking the wheel again

"Shouldn't we wait?"

Xavier suggested that the boat would be taken by the current long before the coast guard arrived to investigate. He usually found them either incompetent or corrupt (or both) anyway—police in general. For the first time I felt the slightest bit unsafe in his company.

Xavier manoeuvred his much larger yacht to a position alongside the abandoned one. The flat water and the lack of wind allowed him to easily maintain the short distance between the two boats. He left me with control of the wheel, the engine now in neutral. Orion's hull was much higher in the water than the smaller boat's hull, but even so Xavier was able to step on board with little effort. He secured his dock line to the mid and aft cleats of the other yacht and disappeared into its cabin below. I held my breath.

The tension rose when Xavier reappeared carrying a body over his shoulder. I could tell the figure was a man, but I couldn't tell if he was alive. The man was dressed in black pants and a tight black t-shirt and his hands and feet were bound.

Xavier climbed up to *Orion*'s deck using one hand while the other balanced the bound man on his shoulders. I ran over to help, although I wasn't sure what I could do. Untie the man? As Xavier climbed over the lifelines, he directed me to undo the rope that held *Orion* to the other boat before it could cause any damage. He then asked me to get a large glass of water from the galley. So the guy was alive at least...

Orion drifted from the other yacht the moment I released the line from the cleats. I looked over to see Xavier at the wheel piloting us to a safe distance, the man in black still bound at his feet. I expected Xavier to put the engine back in neutral once we were clear, but instead he cranked it, speeding into the fog. I grabbed the rail to catch my balance.

"What are you doing?" I shouted.

I clambered towards him at the console. We should have been waiting for the coast guard. Undoubtedly they'd have questions. Something wasn't right. Why were we driving the boat's captain away from his ship? I kneeled down to undo the ropes that still tied the man. Xavier grabbed my arms and pulled me away—far away—from the prone figure. I fought Xavier but he held me until I eased off. I looked him in the eyes, furious.

"Why haven't you untied him?" I shouted, panicked.

"I tied him up. Why would I untie him?"

Great. A hard knot took shape in my stomach.

"Why would you tie up another boat's captain?" I challenged, striking at him.

"He is not the captain," said Xavier, averting my blows.

"How do you know?"

"Because I saw the captain," Xavier replied quietly," and he was not alive."

"You're sure?"

"The bullet hole in his head made me sure."

I grimaced, but questioned his conviction that the dead guy was actually the captain.

"So how come he didn't shoot you, too? Did you knock him out before you tied him up?"

"This man," Xavier continued, "was unconscious. But he had a gun in his waistband and death on his hands. He is not a good man."

We both turned and looked back at the unconscious figure on the deck. He was ugly, and scarred, but that didn't mean he was bad.

"We should hand him over to the police, then." I argued. "Let them figure out who was on the boat and who did what. We shouldn't be moving away with the only witness!"

"Perhaps, but the police are corrupt," mused Xavier, which was annoying. He turned his head away and mumbled, barely audibly, "Also, I know this man."

"You know this man? How could you know a man we just found in the middle of the Ocean?"

"I don't know how it is possible, but it is true—I have met him before, and he is very dangerous. We cannot trust him."

"So he's a disgruntled record exec, then?" I snapped. It was blatantly clear that there was a lot more to Xavier than merely being the owner of a small record label. "Idiotic," I reminded myself of my risky decision to join him—and now I was paying for my mistake.

Xavier shot me a hurt glance and said he couldn't get into it right now. He moved away from me and back to the wheel of the boat which had begun to turn in a dangerous circle. He straightened us up through the fog, keeping a distance from the figure at his feet as he checked the radar on the console. I sat down on the bench opposite, the knocked-out man between us. Where was the gun now?

Chapter 5

After a long silence the man on the floor of the deck let out a horrible groan. I looked down at him and was startled to see a deep brown pair of eyes fixed on me. 'Help' he mouthed, indicating Xavier with his eyes. Xavier was too busy navigating us through the dense fog to notice. The man held up his bound hands to his mouth, miming drinking. I got up.

"I'm going to get that glass of water," I explained as Xavier looked over at me, questioning. "Do you want anything?"

"No, merci," he replied. He watched me intently with a look of concern, but I would not let it soften me. This was all wrong. I felt myself being swallowed by a black vortex of evil absurdity.

"Are you alright?" He continued.

I shrugged and went below to get the water.

"He doesn't need water now," Xavier said when I returned. "You should drink it, maybe."

I plunked down in my same spot, thinking I'd give it to the guy anyway. I waited for Xavier to be distracted by the navigating. He kept glancing at me, however. I pretended to drink from the plastic tumbler. I would only look down at the man between us when I felt Xavier wasn't looking. The guy was creepy—he had a unibrow over heavy cheekbones and a piece of bridge was missing where a scar cut across his nose. His black stare was chilling. Were those eyes pleading or calculated? They gave nothing away.

Xavier relaxed his attention at last. I leaned over his prisoner to offer the man some water. I know Xavier saw me because he reached out to pull me away a second time.

44

But he wasn't fast enough.

The thug on the floor had his arms up over my head before I knew what was happening. He pressed my neck to his chest in an intense muscular grip. I saw the plastic glass fly off the back of the boat. I pushed against the man to no effect. I could hear Xavier call out my name in alarm. Using his powerful arms the man twisted my head around to face outward. The rest of my body had no choice but to follow suit. My throat was now tight in the crook of his elbow, and he was squeezing my air passage closed. I tried pulling his arm away, tried elbowing him in the ribs, tried just to catch a breath. I vaguely saw Xavier pull out a gun and hold it against the man's head just above my eye line. But I don't know what happened next because I blacked out.

***

When I came to I was lying in Xavier's bed. He was stroking my hair and studying my face intently. He smiled at my open eyes but I pulled away.

"Did you kill him?" I asked. My voice came out as a painful, hoarse whisper.

"No...I hit him over the head. Hard," he explained, handing me a nearby glass of water. He seemed amused by my question.

"It's not funny," I said. "I don't know what you're capable of."

"No, it's not funny," he sighed. "It's not funny what he did to you. It's not funny what he did to that sailor. And it's not funny that you think I am that type of man to kill him."

"So where is he?"

"I locked him in the starboard v-berth. He has a big lump on his head, but he will be alright."

"You said you knew him."

Xavier's shoulders sank. It was not typical of his usual confident body language. He rubbed his face for a moment, sorting out where to start, and how much to divulge. He sighed, and looked me in the eye.

"He is a goon who works for a Liberian diamond

smuggler."

"Ha!" I shot a rasping accusation at him. "That's ridiculous!"

"That may be," he shrugged. "But it is true."

"But how do you *know* someone like that?"

"Before I started my label," he continued with some hesitation, "I worked to recover stolen art. Mostly very expensive art. The diamond smuggler, he was a large collector. His favourite was l'expressionnisme abstrait. That never—"

"You were a police detective?" I cut in.

It was my turn to be amused.

"No, I worked privately. I investigated with the aid of Interpol but my clients... sometimes they wanted more attention paid to them. They were able to fund investigations without the trouble of bureaucracy. And I had been friends with many of them all my life."

"The Swiss bankers."

"Oui. Et leurs amis."

"That explains why you might be playing high-stakes poker with a drug lord from Zanzibar."

"Goldfinger..." he smiled at some private memory. "Always one step ahead of me—I never caught him with the Cezanne he had bought. I think that this yacht was for a retirement gift for me. He knew that I was thinking that I would stop working. But, if I had lost the hand he would have taken the kidney out immediately and left me to die."

"Did you say he *bought* the Cezanne?"

"Stolen art trades many hands. I didn't always recover articles from the original thieves."

"That must have pissed off some nasty people."

"Yes, it did. I decided that it was the time to retire when that bastard in there murdered my brother and his wife."

I had no idea what to say. Xavier didn't notice, being preoccupied with the heavy ghosts of his past.

An uncomfortable realization crawled over my skin.

"You knew he was going to be out here, didn't you?" I accused him, convinced I already knew. "That's why you're taking this trip."

Xavier began to shake his head but the red shame of his cheeks beat his denial to the punch.

"It was . . . I heard…," he choked on the truth. "I only knew that he was possibly in the area. It's not why I am sailing. My trip was planned long before. But I knew also that it was a small chance… The ocean is big but irony always plays a strong hand."

"And you brought me with you anyway, knowing how dangerous it could be?" my voice cracked.

"I did not expect this, even after I had handed you over to safely to your uncle, I did not expect to find this man. I… I am very sorry," Xavier muttered. He would not look at me.

"And what now? If you are not a killer, and you won't call the police?" I rasped, furious still. He turned back and faced the challenge of my glare.

"I owe a debt," he said.

He turned away to leave, but not before I caught a wave of pain move like a shadow across his face. When he looked back from the doorway to suggest I get some more sleep, the shadow was gone.

***

I dreamt of a thousand dolphins swimming in a river of moonlight. Their silver bodies sparkled with phosphorescent wakes. At the head of the pod was a large black dolphin. The Dolphin King. He had a nose for trouble. Bits of garbage drifted in the sea ahead. As we approached the pieces became more distinct. I could now clearly make out the shapes of body parts—arms, heads, calves with feet, a head. I saw the face of the head—it was Xavier. His eyes were open and staring at me, cold.

***

I woke with my heart racing, my throat remembering the

death-grip.

There would be no more sleep for me. I wrapped my sarong about myself and went to find something to eat. I headed to the bathroom first. I shivered at the image staring back at me from the mirror. Two patches of bruises framed my neck on either side. I arranged my hair over them to help hide their ugliness.

I eyed the closed v-berth door as I made my way to the galley. There was neither sound nor light leaking from the narrow vent at its base. I shuddered and turned away from the cabin.

I grabbed an apple from the fridge.

The fog had burnt away and the huge sails were up, propelling the boat steadily through rolling waves. Xavier was still setting the sails, going back and forth from the cockpit console to the various sheets to adjust them by hand. His arms rippled as he cranked the winches to pull the sails in or let them out. I was surprised he wasn't just using the automatic winches. Maybe he needed the distraction.

I sat in the cockpit while he worked, but didn't say anything.

The sun was already going down.

Xavier broke the silence to tell me he didn't want me doing a watch that night. His plan was to pull most of the sail in and to sleep out in the cockpit. He'd have an alarm set while he slept, to wake him every 20 minutes. I protested but the hoarse croak of my voice felled any possible argument.

I ate the pasta he offered when the apple proved too painful to swallow. Later I went back to the state room to lie down. I couldn't sleep so I grabbed the cover off the bed, and returned to the cockpit. He watched me with raised eyebrows as I made myself a nest in the lounge area and crawled into it.

At some point he crawled in with me. He held me tight until morning. I slept so well that I never noticed whenever he got up to check the boat.

***

A stronger wind and bigger waves rocked us awake at

sunrise. We let out the big fore-sail and the wind pulled the bow forward, cutting through the waves in a slow, nodding rhythm. We moved with its rhythm as we made our way down into the galley area to make ourselves coffee.

I leaned on the end of the counter at the near end, watching Xavier work his habitual magic with the ship's little cappuccino machine. He stole a long glance in my direction as he waited, hypnotized and hypnotic, for the espresso to drip from the machine.

"I think that you will not want to make love with me again," he said, remorseful.

His comment was a true reflection of how I felt. Whatever delights had developed in the first few days, there was no ignoring the fact that he'd now put me at risk. I continued to be at risk as long as there was a killer on board—a killer he had taken prisoner. And what did he intend to do with him? Xavier's past, once revealed, had ripped my sense of him from a world I was familiar with and flung me into a John Le Carré novel.

I glanced at the locked cabin door at the far end of the galley. I thought I heard noises, shuffling and fidgeting, coming from behind it. It was hard to tell if I was imagining them amongst the other creaking noises of the yacht. I turned back to Xavier who had not taken his eyes off me. The expression on his face was one of regretful resignation. There was a weight to it that carried far more than just the thoughts of our recent intimacy.

"I must take some food to him," he said, not moving. I offered to put something together in the meantime for Xavier and I to eat, and he nodded, thankful.

The rest of the morning proceeded without interruption by disturbing events. Xavier and I hung out in the sunlit cockpit, enjoying the wind in our hair as if it were blowing away our troubles. We watched the sky closely, as the weather faxes were predicting possible storms ahead. We filled our conversations with talk about our favourite comic heroes Asterix and Tintin. We had a very serious discussion regarding the influence Hergé had had on our respective world views as children.

"Bianca Castafiore taught me history," I confided.

He laughed harder than he needed to at that, but I understood. The cloud which hung over us was less apparent when we distracted ourselves with desperate amusements. We clung to any sense of normalcy.

Midway through the day Xavier excused himself and went forward to the bow of the deck to spend a significant amount of time in private calls on his satellite phone. He explained later that he had a contact in Cabo Verde whom he trusted to take care of the gangster below. Xavier told me a little more about the man with the unibrow—more than I wanted to know.

The thug called himself the Scarab, but most people just referred to him as the Scar. He had been involved in trafficking women from Eastern Europe before landing himself a position in the more lucrative illegal diamond trade. Xavier was convinced the man still had a hand in human trafficking, but didn't elaborate on his suspicion. The smuggler the Scar now worked for used him mostly as a long-arm heavy because he hadn't proven to be much of a team player. The man was also known to have a particular knack for disappearing.

"Any chance he'll disappear off your boat?" I asked hopefully.

"Not before killing us," had been the disappointing reply.

Thick clouds accumulated on the horizon in a threatening mountain of monster mash potatoes. Xavier went in to get his daily French net fix and update our information on the weather.

I could just see the back of his shoulders and head at the nav-station from where I sat in the lounge area of the cockpit. He had told me that he played a lot of European football and tennis, and attributed any fitness on his part to those two games alone, but I imagined instead his climbing over the bougainvillea-clad estates of smuggling barons to reclaim stolen treasures. It was so easy to picture him dressed in the tight black outfits that clever thieves wore in movies, the kind that would have accentuated his perfect form.

I went inside to the nav-station where Xavier sat hunched over his notes, occasionally speaking French through the hand-held mic. He kept one eye on me as I moved behind the chair. My fingers traced the shape of his shoulders across the top of the hi-tech seat. His skin was silky and warm to the touch. His hair was tousled but soft. I wound my arms around his bare shoulders and buried my face in his neck. I licked it. He laughed but when I caught his glance his eyes were full of sorrow.

I made myself comfortable on his lap, and accepted an absent caressing from him as he spoke to the other French cruisers. They exchanged information about wind speed, and recommended sail positions. They gossiped about the best wine to eat with fresh caught tuna. Someone had swum with sharks. Xavier didn't mention that we had one locked in our cabin.

We emerged later to discover the grey areas at the base of the thunderheads extending all the way to the water in patches. It was a stunning sight. The rain was so thick it left an impression as a physical landmark as solid as an island. If we were lucky, we might pass through the gaps between the dark masses.

We weren't so lucky.

A spitting rain began to fall as the dark grey mountain blotted out the sun. Xavier turned *Orion*'s engine on before we raced to reef the main sail and pull in the head sails. The drops became heavy and thick as the last triangular tongues of sail slipped around the stays at the front of the yacht. We were both soaking wet and tense. The wind had picked up considerably, making the seas much choppier than they had been moments before.

"Would you grab the rain gear?" Xavier shouted over the wind while he struggled with the zippers of the canvas dodger.

I indicated our dripping selves with my free hand, wondering what the point was.

"And the harnesses?" he added.

Right—didn't want to fall overboard.

We spent the rest of the storm knocking and sliding against each other in the cockpit as the boat tossed us around more than usual. We huddled together at the wheel, protected from the wind by the sturdy canvas shelter of the dodger. The autopilot kept us on track with Xavier making minor adjustments according to the direction of the gusts under the cloud. An hour later it was over.

The sun burst through a cloud abruptly at the end of the storm. Tearing off our wet raingear we found ourselves gawking at a giant rainbow against the now retreating storm. Xavier went down to the state room to grab us some towels. We put the sails back up, turned the motor off, and had dinner in the nude as the cockpit dried under the sharp sun.

The sun set on a smoother sail, the boat's slow, heavy rhythm lifting and dropping us over the wide eight foot rollers beneath us.

Things felt almost normal by nightfall as we returned to our regular watch pattern. I thought I heard banging coming from the bow area at one point but I couldn't be sure as the wind always seemed to play tricks on the ears. The stars shone in full force by the time my second watch came around. A new moon was barely visible, rising in the early dawn sky.

That day a full-blown argument erupted between Xavier and "the Scar." I could hear their muffled yelling through the walnut paneled door of the V-berth. Xavier had been careful to keep the contents of the cabin from view. I felt like Bluebeard's wife, fighting her temptation to open the forbidden door. The memory of that calculated stare from under the unibrow, and the continued soreness of my throat, kept my curiosity in check.

Xavier emerged from the room looking worn and exhausted. He was battling ghosts that had taken on physical form. He hardly noticed me in the galley as he made his way outside, absently massaging his cheeks. I followed him out, and from the cockpit watched him pick his way to the tip of the bowsprit at the front of the yacht. He stayed there for a long time, his legs absorbing the motion bouncing him up and down over the waves while his arms held tight to the gold rails hugging him at both sides.

For the remainder of the day the Scar hurled brutal strings of obscenities at us through the locked cabin door. I say 'us' as I didn't think he was calling Xavier a 'whore'. The voice grew hoarse as the evening progressed until it died in the night after a last rasping grunt.

Xavier, as usual, took the first watch of the night. He pulled on his rain gear and harness with little enthusiasm. I gave him a light kiss on the cheek which seemed to help a little. I made my way down below to the state room and slid under the covers of the large bed to get what sleep I could.

***

Thump. Thump. Thump.

My eyes snapped open. I was sure I had heard a noise, but on listening there was nothing. It was almost too quiet. My tension grew until the normal sounds of water rolling along the sides of the hull and the invading whispers of wind slowly made themselves apparent.

I must have drifted off again as I found myself floating in the waves, bounced by a heard of dolphins that surrounded me. I felt one lift me under its nose and toss me into the sky like a beach ball. I flipped over and over.

I landed awake. This time I definitely heard it.

Bang. Bang. Bang.

It sounded each time the boat rolled to port. The thud was loud enough that it was going to keep me awake, so I got up to investigate. I grabbed my shorts and a t-shirt from the bed and slid them on over my otherwise naked self. I didn't have to go far before discovering the source of the noise. The door to the small V-berth cabin swung open and then slammed shut with every wave that rocked the boat. I tried to catch a glimpse of Xavier's prisoner through the swinging door but it would close again before I got a good look. Why was the boat tossing so violently? I listened to the other noises—a slapping of water against the hull, the breaking of distant waves, the halyards clanking against the mast, overpowered by an intense flapping of canvas. It wasn't another storm. We weren't moving at all.

Chapter 6

My heart beat in my throat. I looked up over the low wall through the nav station to see if Xavier was visible in the cockpit—surely he would have heard the banging? It was dark outside and I couldn't see him. I began to creep back through the galley towards the bow, where a dark chasm was opening and shutting with every toss of the boat.

The lights weren't on in the tiny berth, but there was enough light leaking from the galley to reveal one important factor: the berth was empty. The ropes which had held Xavier's prisoner lay on the floor of the room, frayed cuts just visible in the faint light. There were dark stains on the floor as well. The cabin smelled like vomit, and piss. My incredible fear was tinged with sympathy. The sympathy wouldn't last.

I turned and ran the length of the boat, up the stairs through the upper cabin lounge to the empty cockpit outside. Where was Xavier?

The boat lurched and I grabbed the console quickly before falling over. Someone had cut all the lines to the sails, leaving them flapping wildly in the night air. The boat had turned into the wind, but the big yacht was essentially useless. *Orion* was nothing more than a cork being tossed by the ceaseless rollers. I saw a dark shape rolling on the deck ahead, knocking against the life lines. One arm dangled dangerously over the gunnels, saltwater lapping at the fingers. I knew that figure...

"Xavier!"

I picked my way along the unstable deck towards him. The occasional wave sprayed me as it broke against the hull. I heard a groan when I finally reached him. I knelt down, clutching the lifelines with one hand while I shook his shoulder and called his name.

He jolted awake, grabbing hold of me to pull himself up. He almost took us both overboard. Neither of us was wearing a harness or a lifejacket. Xavier should have been wearing one during his watch. I pushed him down against the combing, away from the grasping waves. He struggled to collect himself and at last his awareness returned. He looked up at me, still anxiously holding my arm tight.

"Are you alright? Safe?" He had to shout to be heard over the sails flapping in the dark wind above.

I nodded. "Are you?" I yelled back.

"What happened?" Did Xavier not know?

"He's gone," I cried.

Xavier looked at me like he didn't know what I was talking about. It only took a moment for it all to come back. I could see his mind racing back into high gear.

After a quick inspection of the ruined rigging, he indicated we should get off the deck. Once we were safely in the cockpit he raced ahead of me to the nav station inside. He couldn't find the item he'd run for, and was now looking around frantically. He began to swear loudly and finally flicked on the lights. That's when I saw the blood running down his back from an injury somewhere on his head. I gasped.

He turned to see what had scared me and kept turning when that caused him to completely lose his balance. I managed to catch him as his knees buckled, and I guided him to the space-age chair. He put his head between his legs while I grabbed some towels from the galley kitchen. I held one against the back of his head where it was now brutally evident he'd been struck.

"He has taken the satellite phone," Xavier grimaced through gritted teeth.

I reminded him that we still had two working radios, and could call for help. He clarified that wasn't the problem. Wherever the Scar had disappeared to, he was now capable of making calls, and that worried Xavier—with a satellite phone the Scar could contact the people he worked for, and we remained a target so long as we remained inert.

"Did he take the dinghy?" Xavier mumbled from under the towel.

Neither of us could remember seeing the dinghy hanging in its usual spot out on the stern. I went to look and came back moments later to confirm it was gone. I was happy. The creepy unibrow had disappeared and we were both still living.

I cleaned Xavier's head wound as well as I could and washed the blood from his back. I made tea which he scoffed at but drank anyway. He spent the momentary lull deep in thought and apologized for the lousy passage he'd given me.

"Just get us out of this," I said.

Xavier recommended we motor until daylight when he would attempt to re-rig the sails. We put on our safety harnesses and went back out on deck to deal with the flapping sails in the meantime.

We furled the head sails and dropped the main. The thunderous slapping sound subsided, replaced by the slow rushing thunder of the waves nearby and the various creeks and clanks of the boat as she tossed in them.

Xavier shifted to the console to start up the engine before discovering the key was missing.

"Bâtard!" shouted Xavier, kicking the console.

He closed his eyes for a moment to invite a sense of calm. "I have another," he said softly, squeezing my arm affectionately as he swept past into the cabin. Our precarious situation made it even more critical that we watch for other boats. Our sailing lights were on, so at least we were visible. I looked around at the dark horizon. There was a faint light to the East. It could have been a star.

Xavier returned with his spare key. He noticed the light in the distance as well, and frowned. He put the key in the ignition and turned it. The engine choked a moment and died. Xavier swore and tried the key again with the same results. He hung his head while drumming his fingers on the console in thought.

The faint light on the horizon had become three: a white

light flanked by a green and a red. The lights suggested that the boat was a freighter heading straight for us at full speed. I just hoped it would be able to see us, because we didn't seem to be getting out of the way anytime soon. If we were really lucky it might even stop and help us.

Xavier lifted his head to gaze at me. He looked really worried. He climbed over the edge of the cockpit to the deck, touching my arm again as he moved passed. I heard him yell from the darkness somewhere. He reappeared, jaw hard.

"He has put something in the tank," sighed Xavier with renewed despair. "We are going nowhere tonight." He dropped into the seat behind the cockpit console. I joined him there and with his arm around me watched the lights of the freighter approach us. We could now make out the shape of it on the horizon.

"It will see us, right?" I meant it as a rhetorical question but it didn't come out that way. The ship was moving fast. Xavier watched it tensely, said the ship definitely knew we were there.

"Isn't this one of those moments when flares might be a good idea?"

Xavier seemed to find my question very entertaining.

"I am thinking," He responded, "that this is a good moment to escape in the life raft and to hope that the coast guard are competent."

We began to make out the sound of the engines of the freighter, a muffled rumbling in the distance.

Xavier left the safety of the cockpit and scrambled across the deck towards the life raft at the bow. He indicated I should follow him but sped on ahead of me—all I could see of him was his pale silhouette. Even so, his disappointment at the latest discovery was evident in his body language. I shared his disappointment in finding the safety shell cracked open, and long savage holes stabbed through the rubber raft inside. It was unusable.

Xavier's no doubt sarcastic comment about our situation was drowned out by the freighter noise. The ship was practically on top of us, dwarfing us. It seemed to have slowed down at least, settling into a position nearby. It was close enough that I thought I might be able to see figures on the decks above, but it was too dark. I maintained my hope that the freighter was stopping to help, but there was an ominous nature to its approach.

"There's something wrong about that ship," I stated over the deafening chug of the freighter. Xavier nodded, and I continued my thought process aloud.

"They haven't made any attempt to contact us by radio. Shouldn't they have done that miles back?"

"Yes, they should have. Also, the spotlight, they – "

He cut himself off, and as he did I heard it too—a tiny buzzing like a mosquito.

Xavier spoke my name with an intensity I had not experienced from him.

"That freighter, it is possibly what I feared, and connected to the Scar. It is possibly part of a smuggling ring. If so, we are in danger. They are not nice people. They do horrible things. They would do unspeakable things with you. You must hide."

"What about you?" I protested. And tried to think of a good spot.

"Please." He urged me back toward to cockpit area, following close behind.

"*Orion* belonged to a drug dealer," he continued in my ear. "There is a compartment big enough for you to fit into, in the head. I will have to show you."

My heart beat heavily, my stomach threatening to crawl into my throat. If they had come all this way to get us, there was no spot on the boat they would overlook—not if they were this determined. Xavier lifted me into the cockpit from behind and raced straight past me into the cabin below. I scampered behind him, trailed by the sound of voices carrying across the water from the approaching dingy.

The smuggling compartment was built into the wall just above the toilet. Xavier stood next to me holding the loose piece of walnut siding that had hidden it, his eyes pleading with me to climb up into the hole. It was not very big. I struggled, even with his help, to manoeuvre myself in backwards. Once I had my arms tucked in, he set the panel back in place apologetically.

The darkness consumed me. I listened to the sound of Xavier's voice as he called for help on the radio. Someone answered his signal and he spoke to them in rapid French. A short pause hung in the air before filling with the sound of the crackling radio as he used the shortwave to send an e-mail. These sounds were smothered by the knocking of a dinghy against the hull and the more threatening sound of muffled voices. The voices grew louder and were joined by thumping footsteps along the deck and through the cabin. The thumping of my heart in the darkness overpowered any of the noises outside my cubby hole.

I recognized the familiar yelling of the Scar drift through the cabin and a subdued version of Xavier's as he shouted right back at him. Xavier's shouting stopped suddenly. Oh, God. The men from the freighter began to turn everything inside out in the yacht. The sounds of banging doors, breaking glass, slamming bodies leaked into my dark hiding place. I could hear someone directly on the other side of me poking and scratching at the wall. Shit, shit, shit.

Sudden light glared in my eyes as the piece of wall pulled away from me. A heavy set man stood in front of the tiny toilet, inches from my face, holding the walnut panel in his hands. His was visibly shocked at finding me stuffed in the wall. Another rougher face appeared behind him. The second man shoved the heavy one aside and reached in to grab me.

"No!" I shouted, vainly attempting to punch at him from my awkward spot.

He had no trouble getting a good hold of my arms and dragging me out of the smuggling hole. My legs bounced off the head as they came free of the compartment. I didn't have any time to get my balance before the man hauled me through the cabin to the cockpit. The other men in the cabin—none of whom was Xavier—started yelling in a broken English cacophony about finding "the other one."

The rough guy shoved me ahead of him until we reached the steep stairs up into the cockpit. I thought I might have a chance to break free but halfway up a large hand from outside grabbed the back of my shirt and pulled me up the rest of the way. I didn't see who it was before the lifter had slammed me down on the bench seat face first. I put my arms out to lift myself up but whoever had given me the boost took the opportunity to get a tight grip on my wrists and pull them behind me. They tied them tightly that way. I kicked out blindly at them.

The same callous hands gripped my arms and pulled me up from the bench. The invisible man with the iron grip handed me off to a small Asian guy who was standing beyond the cockpit on the deck. The big guy passed me like I weighed nothing. My flying feet, still kicking madly, occasionally made contact, but more often it was with the boat itself than one of the men who'd boarded her. I stopped kicking so much once I was passed on to the deck. The water next to me threatened like a black and menacing magnet. I heard a familiar voice shout from the bow as I was dragged along the deck towards the freighter's dinghy.

"Tie her feet! Fucking moron."

I spun around the wiry Asian as he tried desperately to push my feet together. I found myself staring at the Scar too closely— the dent in his nose and the bizarre shadow it cast on his face turned my stomach more than anything else I'd experienced so far. He looked me up and down with that cold emotionless stare.

"You're a fucking moron," I spat at him, trying to stand tall. He just laughed at me, and turned his attention to the man at my feet.

"Toss her in dinghy," he growled before moving past me across the combing.

I hoped that meant he had decided to forego tying my feet, but as I looked down towards the dingy I saw the loop around my ankles tighten, throwing me off-balance. I started to fall over the lifelines. The wiry man caught me, but only to realign my fall into the arms of yet another sailor in the dinghy below. And that was when I saw Xavier.

He was lying on the floor of the dinghy, out cold. His arms and legs were bound like mine, and he was bloody. The water in the bottom of the dinghy slapped against his closed face as the boat bounced against the side of the yacht. They lay me on the floor next to him. The weathered rubber was cold and wet, the sea water soaking the few clothes I had on. I called Xavier's name quietly until someone kicked me softly to shut up. Xavier made no response. The worst was easily possible, but I clung to the hope that if he were dead, they would have left him behind. Or simply thrown him into the sea.

The air was filled with sudden rapid shouts and many feet running. The freighter dinghy tossed and knocked as the gang from the yacht climbed on board. I flinched as both I and Xavier were trampled on in the rush. The dinghy jerked forward as the motor spat it away from *Orion*. The shouting continued around us in the boat until it was eclipsed by a huge explosion behind us.

I saw the ball of fire reflected against the surfaces of the dinghy and the legs of the men around us. The roar of the explosion faded fast under the rumble of the freighter engine and the more immediate hum of the dinghy's outboard motor. A few gasps and several hoots and whistles were the only remaining clue that Xavier's well won poker haul was no more.

Chapter 7

The wicked wave bouncing finally subsided as the freighter's black shadow loomed above us. Xavier was still unconscious, the constant jostling of the rough water having done nothing to revive him. His earlier words of warning haunted me. I shivered and hoped that the explosion had been big enough to get the attention of someone who could help us.

One of the sailors had a brief inaudible discussion with the Scar before I found myself being hauled out of the bouncing dinghy and up a long flimsy metal plank that angled to a point high above us. A second sailor joined the first near the top of the gangplank. I caught one last look at Xavier lying prone in the bottom of the little boat before the two thuggish sailors dragged me off the deck into the bowels of the ship.

We passed no one through multiple fluorescent-lit halls and hollow metal staircases. The sailors said nothing, not even to each other. I pleaded with them to untie my feet at least. They ignored me. Bruises formed as my ankles caught on the raised door sills each time we passed into a new section of hallway. At least on the steep stairs one of the sailors would carry my legs.

We stopped and entered one of a series of doors that was indistinguishable from any of the others I'd seen so far. Inside was a small vacant cabin with an unmade bunk, a few hooks on the wall, and a bathroom off to one side. A bare fluorescent bulb fluttered and hummed in the middle of the ceiling. The two men dropped me onto the floor, and left me there. I heard the lock turn behind them.

I wriggled my wrists behind me but there was no give in

the tight binds. The worn linoleum floor was cold, and the parts of my clothes that had gotten wet in the salt water stuck uncomfortably to my goose bump-covered skin. I managed to sit up, with my feet tucked under me. I wasn't as cold once I was off the floor. If only I could just reach the bed…

The sore bruising from the jostling my legs had been subjected to was already showing in places—scattered blue patches around my shins and feet, my thighs. The discomfort of my shins made it difficult to move myself along the floor. The exertion, even as it warmed me up, tired me out. I gave up two-thirds of the way across the room and lay back down on the cold, hard floor.

I waited, shivering, for them to show up with Xavier. What was taking so long? Had they taken him to the ship's doctor instead of locking him in the cabin with me? It seemed unlikely but the alternative—that he hadn't survived—was too daunting to dwell on. I closed my eyes. He would be here soon…

I don't know how I slept, but I was jerked awake by the sound of the lock turning behind me. The door opened and slammed shut. I turned around and found myself face to face with the Scar. He was alone.

"What have you done with Xavier?" I demanded, before he could say anything—before my fear and revulsion could silence me.

"*What have you done with Xavier?*" He repeated in an ugly high-pitched mockery of my distress. He locked the door and turned back to me.

"Forget about that guy. He is dead. We threw him over. He is weak bastard."

He strode across the room towards me. I shrank into the floor. He noticed, but stepped right over me to perch on the bunk behind me. I refused to turn and look at him and otherwise tried to cover my fear. I didn't want him to see any flicker of belief I might show about his horrible news. He was lying about Xavier, I needed to believe that.

"This is what is going to happen," he declared to the back of my head in his heavy Eastern European accent. "The captain does not accept passengers without payment. So, you have to earn passage. Unless you have money? No, I don't think. Lucky, there is many men on board willing to pay for things... favours. You will offer service, they will pay. I must take percentage. And the captain also—he takes percentage. It's not enough, I think, for full passage. So we will see, when we are over, how much you will need to finish paying. You will work for it."

"Fuck you," I replied through the silent tears that spilled over my eyelids.

"Fuck me?" He asked, mildly surprised.

His savagely grabbed a handful of my hair, took hold of one arm and lifted me right off the floor. My bare toes found a precarious foothold as he balanced me upright.

"You have no choice," he spat in my ear. "You work for me, or you go off the ship. Splash."

"Fuck you," I repeated, angrier. I hoped he did not notice I was crying.

It wouldn't have mattered. He lugged me to the door, releasing my head only to unlock the door and open it. He shoved his heavy arm behind mine, so that he had both of my arms in a sandwiching grip against his side. His other hand held my head against his chest by a solid fistful of hair. He carried me like this back the way we had come, along the metal-clad passages. I started screaming.

He bellowed his own rant, against me, against the Frenchman, against all whores, against all humans. He was as loud as my screams for help. Our yelling echoed down the corridors as we turned corners and passed through doorway after metal doorway. The last door exited to an exterior deck. The sky behind the silhouetted railing was changing from a deep violet to a soft mauve. Half the night had vanished.

I struggled with whatever strength I had left, hoping he would drop me before we reached the edge. He gripped tighter and then slammed me hard against the railing at the far side of the deck. Our shouting stopped as the move knocked the air out of both of us. I was hanging halfway over, gulping at the sea air. A hundred feet below black water churned along the side of the huge freighter. All the Scar had to do was lift my bound feet and I would be sent tumbling for a death swim.

"Scarab," interrupted a deep voice from somewhere behind us.

The Scar froze, one hand holding up my legs by the rope that bound them, the other crushing me against the thin metal railing. Sounds of a number of footsteps clanked towards us across the steel-clad deck. The scar's grip on my legs softened, letting them fall to the floor. He took a tight handful of my shirt from the back and pulled me off the railing to a seated position at his feet. He kept a tight grip on me there.

"Captain." The Scar spoke in a surprisingly deferential tone.

The Ship's captain was African, from what particular country I couldn't tell. His English was good, though. The men that surrounded him showed obvious respect, keeping a slight distance back from the conversation between the two men. None of the men looked directly at me. All of the men were dressed in casual clothes, with the exception of the captain, who stood out in a stereotypical captain's hat. He did not seem pleased at the situation.

"Scarab, if anyone is going to throw people overboard from my ship, they are to go through me."

"Yes, sir." The hint of contempt I expected to hear from the Scar seeped into his response.

"Some of the men are disturbed by the amount of yelling. You know it is bad luck to have a woman on board a ship."

They both laughed, but there was an undertone of posturing.

"Perhaps you have lost your touch," continued the captain, subtly more threatening. The grip on the back of my shirt tightened. "And I hear you are making a big mess in my sub-hold. When you are finished your business there I expect it to be cleaned up. Thoroughly."

Xavier was in serious trouble but he was still alive—he was on the ship and breathing.

I wrenched away from the hand that gripped my shirt, but the Scar held fast.

"You asshole!" I shouted at him, shocking everyone out of their complacency. "He's not dead! You—"

The pudgy hand of the Scar smothered my mouth, cutting me off. He lifted me up and held me by the waist tight against himself. He apologized briskly to the unhappy captain and sped with me back down the multitude of empty interior corridors. I continued to rage beneath his smothering gag, kicking against his grip with my bound legs and attempting to bite his hand. Inside the bare cabin he threw me to the floor face down. The heavy landing knocked all the air out of me.

He flipped me over with his foot so that I faced him. I stared up at his cold black eyes, helpless. I had no fight left. Tears were streaming down my cheeks, but they had no effect on him. He undid my shorts, pulling the zipper down far enough to reveal my vulnerable nakedness underneath. He chuckled to himself. A knot of fear gripped my stomach.

"I hate you," I murmured at him.

"Your Frenchman is waste of time," he mused, as if I'd said nothing. "You are not for him," he continued his monologue, working methodically as he spoke. "I know. His brother's wife— she was the one for him."

He pulled a knife from his pocket. I screamed again, sure he was going to slice me up. Instead, he used it to tear a long strip off my shirt which he then forced into my mouth to shut me up.

"She was very beautiful," he went on. "I knew her. The Frenchman fucked his brother's wife. Poor Frenchman's brother. The brother is dead now. The wife is dead, too. But, the Frenchman thinks she is not. Still he is asking for her. Stupid Frenchman. He is in love with a dead whore. He does not ask for you."

He dragged me painfully by the hair across the room to the bunk, and sat me up against the corner of it on the floor. His words burned more deeply than my scalp, but I didn't want him to know that.

He exchanged his knife for a length of cord from his pocket. He used it to tie my neck to the bunk post. The line wasn't tight, but it forced me to sit up tall against the bed frame, or be

66

strangled by the rope. He stood back, nodding and grunting to himself. I glared at him through my tears, unable to scream at him. I thought I had known hate in my life, but that was nothing to the rage I felt towards this monster now.

He hung his coat on one of the hooks behind the door. Then he left, switching the light off behind him. The darkness sank in like the cold, and crept through my skin to fill the walls of this fortress of dread.

How was I going to get out of this?

I felt around behind me. Maybe there was something sharp on the bunk frame that I could use to cut my ropes. The legs of the bunk were round, so that wouldn't work. But maybe a spring or a piece of frame? I couldn't feel around much behind me without leaning forward, which caused the cord around my neck to choke me. I fought back the panic which threatened to set in. I would have to wait for an opportunity.

A thin thread of light teased under the locked door. It was just enough light to make out the few dim shapes in the room—the jacket, a wooden chair, the open bathroom door. Footsteps surfaced through the din of the big freighter. A shadow passed across the crack of light. The footsteps faded. Time passed. It was not a busy corridor.

Other sounds emerged. A distant drip replaced the click of steps. A pipe in the corner of the room flushed with water. The air conditioning kicked in and drowned out everything but my pounding heart. When the air vent went quiet, the drips came back. Another shadow passed by the door.

I shifted my weight when I could. I forced myself to wiggle my fingers and toes to keep them from going numb as my arms and legs began to cramp. I did the same with my shoulders. How long was I going to be left like this? I counted the drips. I stopped when I reached 2000.

I was plagued by worry for Xavier. My only clue about his situation was the Captain's warning…"a mess in the hold." The thought turned my stomach. What were they doing to him? Would he still be alive at this point? How much payback did the Scar need for his few days of captivity? He had already murdered Xavier's brother. And sister-in-law. For whom Xavier still pined.

I counted 15 air conditioning cycles, 12 shadows, and 63 flushes.

I imagined what we would do once we got out of this. I manufactured a beautiful French chateau, surrounded by rolling vineyards that we would frolic in. We would have horses. Famous musicians would come from all over the world to record in the studio we'd build in the chateau. I would take cooking classes. And language classes. And I would paint...

But my imaginings were shattered by thoughts of his being beaten until his bones broke. Or by thoughts of his escaping to find his brother's beautiful dead wife while I was left here to my horrible fate.

If Xavier didn't survive, what would that mean for me? What was the point of keeping me on the ship if it wasn't for the Scar's wicked retribution? Would I be tossed overboard after all? Or was the Scar serious about getting something else out of me while on board? And afterward.

Two shadows passed in front of the crack under the door and stopped. The lock turned and the door burst open to reveal the silhouette of the Scar and a smaller, wiry man. The Scar flipped on the fluorescents and locked the door behind them. The sudden light pained my eyes. I shut them against it. I opened them when I heard the weird sigh of the wiry man. He stared at me with his jaw hanging, transfixed. He could have been the same wiry Indonesian who had handled me on *Orion*. He was an older man, maybe in his 50's.

The Scar stepped between us to block the man's view, holding his upturned palm out to the Indonesian. The wiry old man pulled a crumpled wad of bills and some change from his pocket. He craned his neck around to get another look at me. The Scar counted out the money. He held his hand up, shaking his head. He wasn't happy.

"No touch," insisted the Scar.

The older man pleaded in another language. The Scar was adamant. An argument ensued, much of it via body language. The wiry Indonesian kept pointing at my shirt and touching his chest.

The Scar slashed his arms through the air in an emphatic 'no'. The Indonesian indicated he wanted his money back. The argument repeated until the Scar held up his hand for it to stop. He agreed to a concession.

The Scar took what was left of my shirt in his brutal pudgy hands and tore it wide open from the neck. He yanked the shoulders back to expose my front to his paying customer.

"No touch," he repeated.

The wiry man put his hands together and bowed his thanks to the Scar. The scar stepped back against the wall near his coat and took a seat in the wooden chair.

"Open your legs for him," he barked at me. I growled back at him through the shirt stuffed in my mouth. I kept my legs together.

He was across the room before I had time to cringe. His fat palm struck me across the face, stinging hotly and throwing my head sideways against the cord around my neck. He kicked my knees apart with his rough boots as I coughed through my gag. There wasn't much give even if I had been willing to spread my legs.

The old Indonesian waved his hands in protest, shaking his head and yelling at the Scar to stop. He wanted his money back. That was enough to get the Scar's attention. The Scar scrambled to escort the Indonesian out without a refund. I had a cold feeling that I would be the one who would end up paying. A hairy arm snaked in and shut the lights, plunging me back into the despairing darkness. The last thing I saw was a sad embarrassed—albeit unwanted—glance from the wiry Indonesian elder.

The lock turned and their shadows passed on.

I fought back tears and lost. Huge sobs of helplessness flooded over me. I was alone and desperate. Even if Xavier was alive, he could not protect me from his place in the hold. I had no way to fight. I was never going to cooperate, which left me to be beaten and drugged or tossed into the sea to drown. I would probably be tossed over anyway, after much abuse and humiliation. I wasn't sure how many times I could take being struck across the face. Or worse. I tried to convince myself that I could handle it—somehow. Because there had to be an end to it. Crippled by despair, my state of helplessness was too much for me.

I cried until the shudders had waned to nothing more than weak sighs. I cried for myself and for the loss of Xavier. I was lucky that the gag in my mouth had allowed some air passage. My eyes dried up but I had to keep sniffing or I would have suffocated. The shirt now tasted like tears. My face still burned where I had been hit.

The frequency of passing shadows dwindled to nothing. The deep rumble of the engines underpinned everything, coupled with the high pitch of air-conditioning and fluorescent light humming from the hallway. The cabin I was in must have been fairly high up, as there was no sound of water apart from that which rushed through the pipes in the walls.

My face eventually stopped throbbing. My hunger added to my array of discomforts. I'd passed the point where the walls of my stomach were eating themselves. How many hours had it been since I last ate? What was that asshole going to expect from me before I was given anything to eat?

Chapter 8

The stillness of the ship was interrupted by a flicker in the crack of light under the door. My body tensed, anticipating the sound of the lock being thrown. But the dreaded tumble didn't come. Instead there was the hesitant jangle of the lock being toyed with. The door slipped open with a pop, and the shadow lock-picker slipped inside. The intruder shut the door, turned the lock, but left the light off.

I froze. Who knew I was here? One of the thuggish sailors who'd dropped me off on our arrival? The shadowy figure hobbled closer. He breathed with a heavy rasp. My heart pounded in my ears. I didn't want to give my location away.

Then I heard him speak my name with fearful hesitation.

I moaned back through my gag.

"C'est Xavier," he choked, as if I might not have known for sure. He felt his way to my side in an instant, his hands feeling for the gag in my mouth. They trembled against my skin. I could smell dried blood.

"He said you were dead," I sobbed as soon as my mouth was free.

"I refuse to give him the pleasure," responded Xavier with his characteristic flippancy. "Are you hurt? Has he hurt you?"

I didn't know how to answer that. I didn't want to. I changed the subject.

"How did you get away? How did you know where I was?" I asked instead.

"We have a friend on the ship. He helped me to get free, and he told me that I would find you here."

"A friend?" It was impossible to imagine that word applied to anyone on board.

"Someone who is unhappy. He must have been here because he could tell me where to go. He was older, maybe he is Vietnamese. Or Indonesian?"

I knew exactly who he meant.

"He is no friend," I clarified.

I knew that the older sailor had most likely undermined the Scar out of spite and not out of any friendly feelings towards either of us. I had been so humiliated that I could not bring myself to suffer any gratitude towards him, even if he had just saved our lives.

Xavier's urgency increased when I failed to assure him of my well-being. It was clear he was having trouble breathing. He felt along my shoulders to my arms to determine where I was bound. His hands froze as he passed the cord at my neck, again as he discovered my shirt had been ripped open. His breathing became more laboured and I realized he was crying.

"I'm okay," I said quickly. He was struggling with the knot at my neck when I remembered Scarab's coat.

"Xavier! He left his coat here—there's a knife in the pocket!"

"Où?"

"It's on the wall by the bathroom. Why don't you turn on the light?"

"They will know I am here," warned Xavier. "The bathroom maybe has a light."

He fumbled his way in the dark. A pale bulb lit up a corner of the small bathroom. It also lit up Xavier. I gasped—if I hadn't already heard his voice, I wouldn't have recognized him. The right side of his face was swollen and discoloured. His naked body was covered in blood from head to foot. He cradled a contorted left hand against his chest.

"Oh, God—what did they do to you?"

But Xavier was dealing with his own horror at the sight of me. He raced, badly limping, to where the Scar's coat hung on the wall. Halfway there a noise from the hall interrupted him. There were voices at the door and the sound of the lock turning.

Xavier switched off the bathroom light and dove under the bunk. I heard him stifle his own scream.

The Scar burst in. He was trailed by a huge, rough-looking sailor. They had both been drinking heavily, and leaned on each other for support. The brutal-looking sailor caught sight of me in the shaft of light from the corridor. He let out a hoot and slapped the Scar on the back. He ranted in their native Eastern European tongue.

Unseen, Xavier struggled with the knots around my wrists. He wasn't having much success.

The Scar shut the door behind them, flicking the overhead lights on. Even drunk, he was all business. He began to haggle with his colleague. The big man stopped joking around and brought out a serious wad of cash. He was paying for more than a voyeuristic jerk-off. This was the real thing. I had to make it stop.

"You don't want to fuck me," I interrupted their bargaining. I hoped the Scar was too drunk to think about why I was able to speak. The wad of shirt from my mouth lay in a clump on the dirty floor beside me. I didn't want it stuffed back in.

The two of them stopped talking and turned to me like they'd forgotten I was there. Under the bed I felt Xavier's hand squeeze mine, pleading. What else was I supposed to do? My voice was the only weapon I had.

"I'm full of disease," I continued, ignoring Xavier's caution. The Scar shrugged, said something to the big sailor that may or may not have been a translation of my threat. The big brute laughed it off. He handed the Scar the amount of money they had agreed on. The Scar stuffed it in his pocket. He counted off a number of undecipherable conditions to the sailor, who nodded and shook the Scar's hand. They both turned to me. My stomach threatened to throw up its lack of contents.

The Scar stumbled the three steps to my spot on the floor and undid the cord at my neck. I thought he would undo the others as well, but I was mistaken. He dropped the neck cord to the floor, and left me alone in the room with the sailor.

The moment the door shut the big brute stammered forward

and picked me up off the floor by the shoulders. Without effort, he flung me down on the bunk. I winced as I landed hard on my back, crushing my arms. I pulled my legs in to try to protect myself.

"Stop this!" I cried. "I want you to stop!"

"No Inglich," he admitted, shaking his head. He stepped back to undo his pants.

Was Xavier still under the bed? I knew he would be out here fighting this monster off if he had the chance. Had he not been able to crawl out unseen? Maybe there was something I could do to help him. I just hoped he hadn't passed out.

The giant in front of me was having trouble undoing his belt. He was too drunk to see straight. This was the closest thing to opportunity I might get. I coiled my legs like a spring.

"Hey, stupid," I taunted.

He looked up, dropping his hands from his pants. That left me a perfect target. I kicked my feet out towards him hard, and landed a square hit to his groin.

The sailor doubled over in pain, collapsing to the floor on his knees. He was groaning with fury. And if he turned his head three inches to the left, he would be looking right at Xavier's hiding place. I had to do something to distract him. I swung my legs over to the end of the bed, and scrambled to a standing position. The furious brute had his eyes fixed on me, hungry for his moment to retaliate. I hopped from the bed to keep the sailor's focus diverted from Xavier. Or at least I tried to hop, until I fell flat on my face. But I was away from the bed, and that was all I cared about.

The big sailor howled with ridicule at the sight of me lying prone in front of him. He rose from the floor and stood towering over me. I was terrified, but grateful his back was to the cabin bunk. My gratitude was cut short when an unexpected tongue of fire snaked across my back and arms. He had struck me with his leather belt. I gasped at the pain and tried to wriggle away from him. He stepped after me easily and lashed at me again, this time hitting the back of my legs. I screamed at him to stop. He sniggered and followed with another stinging blow to my back.

His mocking was cut short by a big grunt. The belt dropped

to the floor beside me. I looked up to see Xavier holding his arm across the neck of the big sailor, pulling him backwards away from me. The two men were about the same height, but the sailor was almost twice Xavier's weight. Xavier's advantage came from the piece of cord he had retrieved off the linoleum floor. In short order the sailor was on his knees, grasping at his neck. He tried to shake off his attacker but was growing weaker by the second. Finally he collapsed. Xavier checked the unconscious sailor's pulse. He nodded to himself.

Xavier was finally able to retrieve the knife from the Scar's coat pocket and cut my binds. He massaged my stiff shoulders but I had to stop him when it hurt too much. He helped me up with his good hand, and then limped back to the prone sailor with the cut pieces of rope. I convinced Xavier to let me tie up the unconscious sailor, so that he could go into the small bathroom and try to wash some of the blood away.

I tied the last piece of rope around the legs of the sailor just as Xavier wrapped a soft sheet around me. He had taken the mattress cover off the cabin bunk to give me something to wear. I wore it like a toga and was glad to be rid of the shreds that remained of my shirt. Xavier stole the Scar's long jacket.

He'd cleaned off most of the blood from his face, but it was still swollen and bruised all up one side. There was an ugly gash on his cheek which would probably leave a scar.

"That looks much better," I lied.

"Merci," he said, giving me a tentative squeeze, wincing from the pressure that put on his ribs before whispering, "We must go,"

The Scar had left the door unlocked. I tiptoed after Xavier down the empty metal hallways. Once or twice we had to duck to avoid a lone stroller, but for the most part there was no one. We emerged finally on an outside deck, different from the one I had almost been thrown from. This one was closer to the water. I recognized it as the deck we had arrived at from *Orion*.

The sky was black, with its brilliant scattering of stars. We had missed an entire day. There was no hint of light left in the sky, and the new moon hadn't risen. The only sounds were the low

chug of the big engine, and the rushing of dark ocean water
somewhere below.

A large blue lifeboat was hitched to a frame about halfway
along the deck. The lifeboat had an outboard motor attached, and
there were extra tanks of gas strapped to the railing next to it. The
boat was strung up sideways on a pulley system, and not quite
ready to sail. We found a lever on one of the stands the boat was
secured to. The boat began to drop, but it was incredibly noisy. It
descended slowly as well, but we had no choice. Xavier asked me
to crawl into the boat when he'd lowered it enough to lay flat and
level with the deck. It hung dangerously out over the water. He
passed me the extra gas tanks, which I almost dropped due to the
swinging of the boat on its ropes. Xavier went back and hit the
lever once the extra gas was on board. I mimed the big question of
what he was doing, but he signalled to hang on tight.

The boat lowered faster when I was sitting in it. It swung in
the night breeze—the swing widening as the pendulum factor
increased. I clung to the flaked wooden bench as panel after panel
of rusty freighter wall passed me by. The churning water below
grew exponentially louder. Weren't we in danger of getting sucked
under the hull in this tiny outboard? The life boat was still ten or
fifteen feet above the water line when the downward movement
stopped. I looked up to see Xavier's dark figure sliding tentatively
down one of the long lines towards me.

He arrived with a thud, dropping the last several feet as his
strength finally gave out. The boat lurched as he landed, and
rammed into the side of the freighter. We nearly tipped out. I
wondered why he had stopped so high up until a swell came to
within a few feet of the bottom of the boat.

"What now?" I asked, looking down as the swells crested
below us.

"We must cut the lines," he answered, grimacing at a rush
of pain. He displayed the knife from the coat pocket. I looked at
him like he was crazy. "But first we will start the motor, and we
will make the gas secure."

He handed me a spare rope that had been tucked under the
bow. He wobbled past me to the motor and I lugged the tanks of

gas to the underside of the forward bench, wrapping the rope through the tank handles and around the wooden seat. I tied the knot as tight as I could but it was difficult to see. The night was so dark and most of the available light was coming from high above on the freighter. I looked up the dark wall of the ship every so often half expecting to see faces far above. Or guns. A sputter started up behind me. Xavier tested the throttle on the outboard—it wasn't very powerful but it seemed steady. He let it idle.

He tottered back to the bow, checking the security of the gas tanks on his way by. He sliced at the bow line that held us up at the front. He stopped when the rope started to give and we felt the boat slip forward.

"Hang on to the bench," he insisted, indicating I should grip it with both arms. He returned to the stern and braced himself at the bench with his good leg. Then he cut at the stern lines with his good hand. The lifeboat's stern slipped down with a jerk, leaving us hanging at an awkward angle. Xavier looked at me expectantly, waiting for a sign I was ready. I shrugged my shoulders in his direction and gripped the bench tighter. We would be lucky to land upright.

He watched the next roller come in, and when the timing seemed right he gave a swift slice through the last of the stern line. We swung like monkeys for a brief moment before the weighted movement of the boat snapped the chafed bow line. The front end dropped just as the swell crested below us, tipping us away from the churning waters along the base of the freighter's hull. Xavier hit the throttle hard to spin us away from the freighter's dangerous wake.

When it seemed hopeful that we were out of danger, and no gunfire followed us into the dark, Xavier asked if I could take over at the motor. I was happy to do so, considering how pale he was. He snuggled up against my legs, and laid his head on my lap. I found a comfortable position on the stern bench but I had no idea where we were going.

"Xavier," I interrupted his nodding off.

"Hmmm?" he asked without lifting his head.

"Which direction am I pointing the boat in?"

"The one we are going in," he responded, again without looking.

"How do I know it's the right one?"

He laughed, and sat up a moment to point out the constellations I should follow. Some of them he made up at the spur of the moment, like the Kanye West.

"Keep that one directly behind us," he advised. "Africa is to the east. I am hoping."

We'd been on the freighter for a full stretch of daylight and however many hours of darkness. Was it a full 24 hours? I didn't know. Neither of us had any idea which direction the freighter had sailed in once we were on board. It had come from the east, and all we could do was hope it had returned in that direction. With no food, water, or shelter on board, we would only last out here for a day or two. We crossed our fingers that the gas would last that long.

The ocean rollers dwarfed our small lifeboat. We bobbed between them as each one rose and fell. The motor sputtered and skipped at the top of each wave, seeking to grab onto something with which to propel us forward. We would sink with a lurch over the top, the bow slapping the surface of the water just beyond.

My arm was growing numb.

"Are you feeling ok to take over again?" I asked, worried at how still he'd been.

He nodded, still half asleep. I let the throttle slip to neutral. The boat was a lot less stable without the forward momentum, but we managed to switch places. He pulled part of the mattress cover over me as I curled up at his feet. "… To protect you from the wind," he said.

I was so tired that even the jerking and slapping didn't keep me awake. The rhythmic rolling stopped at one point when Xavier changed the gas tanks. I hoped we were at least a third of the way there. I nodded off again.

Xavier asked me to take over when we were halfway through the third tank. I traded places with him and wrapped the mattress cover over the two of us for warmth. The wind tried to tear off our meagre shelter as I clung to the throttle. Somehow I managed to win the tough battle.

A few hours later my arms felt stiff and frozen. My fatigue lifted when I noticed I could make out more detail in the waves around us. The sky was tinged with light ahead of us. A thick line rested on the horizon. I shook Xavier awake. He groaned at the movement.

"Land!" I shouted at him.

He struggled up painfully as the boat continued to rise and fall over successive rollers. He visibly brightened at the sight of the landmass in the distance and turned and hugged my knees in excitement from his cozy spot on the floor of the boat.

"Maybe four hours away at the most," he declared. "Let us hope that it is not Liberia!"

He fell asleep against my lap before I could ask him to take over. I shifted over and drove with the wrong hand instead. The technique was awkward but doable.

The dark line grew. The land lay fairly low, and therefore it was difficult to make out anything identifiable on the horizon. No boats ventured out this far from shore, but I expected to see some as we got closer. I could make out a pale line along the edge of the water that indicated a beach. Small dark patches interrupted the line in places. Was that a sign of civilized life?

Xavier took over at the throttle as the sun rose behind the crisp coastline before us. He followed the shore, riding the incoming waves like a surfboard. The engine sputtered as it gobbled what was left of the last tank of gasoline. We steered the boat towards a cluster of large nets ahead of us, noticing a handful of men standing around them. The fishermen watched us with weary stares but made no move to approach when we landed.

We beached the boat at a polite distance, and tied it off to a nearby shrub. I looked instinctively to sea for any signs of freighters on the horizon. The glinting waves carried nothing but the few small fishing boats that had started out from shore.

I rearranged my mattress cover so that it hung like a toga again. Xavier had pulled his arms out of the Scar's overcoat sleeves and tied the loose pieces around his waist like a belt holding up a skirt. We picked our way across the beach to the fishermen. Xavier had his bad hand cradled at his side. He walked—limped—slightly ahead of me and in the growing light the welts and bruises that covered his back were beginning to put on a real show.

"Bonjour," Xavier called as we got within shouting distance of the fishermen. I was surprised they didn't run for cover—we must have looked incredibly suspicious. A couple of men broke away from the main group and met us halfway.

Xavier initiated bargaining immediately, leaving the fishermen no opportunity to ask questions. They couldn't comprehend his French so instead he indicated the boat to them and mimed painting it. The two men shook their heads, laughing at us as they looked us up and down. One of them called to an older fisherman on the far end of the beach.

"Amadou!" They waved him over.

We watched while the older man trudged across the sand to meet us.

The older fisherman wore a well-loved Baltimore Orioles t-shirt. The solid muscles under his shirt suggested a man in good shape, despite his age. His hair was neatly trimmed and his clothes were clean and mended. He wore sandals, unlike many of the other men on the beach. His skin was deep dark chocolate like the others, but his hair had turned sandy grey.

The two men reiterated Xavier's offer to the old man in another language, presumably the local tongue of wherever we had landed. They gestured and grinned as they told the story, then left the old man to ponder our offer while they went back to work on the nets.

The old man inspected the lifeboat. It was surely clear to anyone with half a brain that we weren't the true owners. We hoped that boats were crucial to survival on the coast, however they were come by. After the boat passed inspection, it was our turn to be scrutinized. The man's big clear eyes took in everything—my lack of clothing, the evidence of violence. His mind grasped at the possible reasons for our dilemma.

The man nodded to Xavier, while squinting out to the empty brightening horizon.

Amadou began to talk in broken French. I watched Xavier's conflicted face light up at hearing his own language then fall as the old man shared an unsettling report. Xavier looked at me to see if I had understood the gist of the conversation. I hadn't.

"He is telling me our arrival is not the first bad omen for the village this morning," Xavier translated as Amadou stood by. "Word has come from the fishermen in another village along the coast that a body, a man, was found on the beach…"

"Is it—?"

"I don't think that there is a connection. He doesn't know anything else, but he says that is why the other fishermen don't speak with us. He says he is not so superstitious."

Xavier's look gave away his true gut feelings about the story. But he smiled to try to ease my worry and turned back to Amadou with a shrug and a grim shake of his head.

Xavier and Amadou began to talk, in French, and quickly warmed up to each other. I caught a few words here and there: that we had landed in coastal Senegal as hoped, that we needed therefore to get to Dakar, that someone was chasing us, that someone had stolen me. I raise my eyebrows at Xavier as the two of them discussed me. I heard the word 'love' and watched Xavier shake his head and indicate himself. Whatever he said seemed to cement their bond. The fisherman continued, indicating Xavier's wounds, and gestured for us to follow him.

The elder fisherman shouted to two young boys as we turned from the beach. They stopped kicking their football around and immediately ran for the boat. They dragged it out of the water and through the trees off the beach. I grabbed one last look at the empty horizon before catching up to Xavier and our new friend.

"What did you tell him?" I asked Xavier, as we fell into a crippled stroll behind our guide.

"He thought that I had stolen you from your angry husband," Xavier replied. His surprise at my question suggested he had forgotten my French was far from perfect. "I explained that it was the other way around."

"He thinks we're married?"

"Yes, but he did not understand why I would want you

81

back."

"He asked you if you loved me…"

Xavier considered my words for a minute. His careful look left me feeling guilty for asking. My emotional vulnerability seemed petty given our current situation. We had more immediate concerns, but my curiosity was burning. I tried to return his studied gaze with my own look of complete nonchalance.

"I felt that he would have more respect for me if I said that it was a matter of pride," responded Xavier finally.

"I guess, but…" I trailed off, not really happy with his answer.

"But?" He was fighting a smile.

"But what about respect for me, too? Why didn't you just tell him I was taken against my will or something. Now he'll think I cheated on you!"

Xavier laughed out loud, and took my hand in an effort to appease my anger. I had never told him the details of my break-up. He had no idea of my brittle sensitivity to infidelity.

"You will find," chuckled Xavier, "that many African men think that it is the nature of women to cheat. Je ne sais pas pour quoi. But when he is less likely to ask many questions that I cannot answer, I will tell him that you did not want to leave my side."

Chapter 9

We passed through the small shrubs that lined the edge of the beach. A dirt road stretched ahead of us, sandwiched by a series of rough concrete buildings. Many of the front yards were enclosed by neat fences made of sticks. Some yards were bigger than others, but each contained a garden and an assortment of chickens. Every dark face froze in fascination as we hobbled past after our elderly guide. We had not gone far when he turned in to one of the larger yards and led us through a non-descript doorway into a cool concrete block box.

The house was sparsely furnished, but its walls were filled with art and other family items collected over many years. Curtains made from vibrant colourful patterns hung on the tiny shuttered windows. A wide piece of fabric hanging from a branch of wild wood separated a small sleeping area from the main room. Two single beds were visible just beyond.

A younger woman came through a doorway at the back. She stopped still in her tracks when she saw us. She stared from the old man to us and back to the old man, then began a long ramble in the village dialect we'd heard on the beach.

The old man held up his hand and the rant stopped. He directed her to take care of Xavier and requested, using gestures as well as words for our sake, that she serve us tea and food. She rolled her eyes and waved her arms and renewed her non-stop talking. Her voice bubbled with a musical tone this time, accompanying her animations.

She took Xavier's good arm and led him to the doorway, beckoning me to follow. Outside we found ourselves in a large treed yard surrounded by more stick fencing and the concrete block walls of neighbouring homes. The yard spilled into a communal area. A number of people, mostly women and small children, were working and playing in the various adjacent spaces. They all dropped what they were doing and wandered over to the yard we sheltered in.

Our hostess ignored her neighbours and guided Xavier to a bench near an open fire pit in the centre of the yard. She continued to ramble musically to us or to herself while the other women grew bored and the children grew more curious. She inspected Xavier's wounds, causing him to wince several times. She 'tsk'ed him and called him a baby—that I understood. I laughed out loud and drew the woman's attention to me for the first time. She grinned but the grin faded fast when she saw me surrounded by the gaggle of curious children. They all tugged at my quilted yellowing toga that was clearly nothing more than a mattress cover.

She yelled loudly and raised her arms in threat. The kids ran off screaming with delighted fear—even I was scared. She burst out laughing, shaking her head, her big grin back on her face. She felt the cover material between her fingers and mumbled in dismay. She told Xavier, in rough French, to 'stay there'—like he was planning on going anywhere. She led me inside the house behind the curtain to the cordoned-off bedroom.

Given the two single beds here, I surmised that she must be the daughter rather than the wife of the fisherman who had accepted our boat. Along the back of the curtain were open shelves containing a number of clothes—t-shirts, pants, and miscellaneous items of bright colour.

She pulled some items off the top shelf and held them up against me. She seemed satisfied with the size, although she was much bigger than I was. She nodded and cheerfully urged me to follow her back outside. I hoped she wasn't suggesting I dress in front of the neighbours. The house would have given me privacy, even if the old man had returned while I was dressing behind the curtain. But she walked past Xavier—whose eye I caught with a shrug—straight to a stick enclave which stuck out from the house. A hose hung down from the roof, attached above to a large drum which sat precariously on some rough 2 x 4 framing. The floor of the enclave had been tiled with concrete block. I noticed an ant-encrusted cake of soap resting on an additional concrete block against the wall. She was offering me a shower. And everyone could see me.

Our hostess noticed my apprehension and began to tug off my shred of privacy. I fought her, but she took my hands and her ongoing rambling developed a soft tone. I gave in and once she had the mattress cover off she hung it up around the fencing to create a fabric wall for me. She rested the change of clothes on the fence as well and then showed me the rusty hose trigger and the ant-encrusted soap. She returned to caring for Xavier.

The shower felt great, despite the frigid morning water. I winced out loud when I accidentally sprayed the cold water against the welts on my back and legs. The skin of my bruised calves blossomed with the same horrific colour as Xavier's back. I took greater care in washing them.

The water drained easily around the edges of the concrete tile. It carried away all the filth and bad taste of the freighter. I turned the hose off as soon as I was rinsed, but found nothing with which to dry myself. The hot African air took care of the dampness—I was dry before I could poke my head out to ask for a towel. I was going to have to be very mindful about my skin under the burning sun.

I jumped when I found my naked self face to face with our hostess. She gestured that I should turn my back to her, and I instantly felt a soothing paste being slathered over the welts on my back. She cooed at me, and disappeared just as magically as she had appeared.

I pulled the bright clean change of clothes off the fence to see what I would be wearing for the next foreseeable while. The hand-made dress slipped easily enough over my head. It was brilliantly coloured and woven at the seams in a simple pattern. It had absolutely no shape to it whatsoever. She had also given me a piece of matching fabric, which I wasn't sure what to do with.

I emerged from the fenced in area with the spare fabric in my hand and padded in my bare feet back to the campfire. The air filled with howls of laughter the moment our hostess saw me in her clothes. Her laughs echoed around the courtyards behind the houses as one after the other of her neighbours looked over to see what was so funny. The high-pitched shrieks of the kids added to the musical laughter of the women as the young ones ran around and laughed at their mothers, and at me. Our hostess beckoned me over once the excitement had died down, but I was distracted by what I was seeing with my own eyes.

Xavier was completely naked. He had been getting a sponge bath while I showered. The Scar's coat sat neatly folded on the other end of his bench, and only a small drape of cloth covered him at the top of his lap. The blood had been washed away and his ribs bandaged by bright white fabric. The slash along his cheek had been roughly stitched closed, but it was clean and cared for. His still-wet skin glistened in the light of the sun. His good eye shone at me—his other eye remained swollen shut.

The fisherman's daughter wrapped Xavier's broken hand in a splint, under his direction. She had straightened his fingers so that his outstretched hand lay against a make-shift board. He would need a proper cast as soon as possible. Some of the moisture on his skin must have been sweat. His hand must be hurting like hell despite the stillness of his face.

"We have had a nice conversation about you," recounted Xavier in his resplendent nakedness.

"About me?" I asked, dubious.

"Oui, bien sur. Astou is very curious about you."

"Astou?"

Our hostess took the cloth from my hand when I reached the bench, and draped it around my waist. She tied it tightly thereby giving me the shape I was missing. She tugged at my arm, nodding in Xav's direction. She was complimenting me on my taste. I returned her grin.

"Her name is Astou," interrupted Xavier, embarrassed.

"Astou," our hostess repeated, pointing at herself. We shook hands.

She gave Xavier another quick appraisal, and disappeared into the dark interior of the concrete block home. I sat beside

Xavier, and let him take my hand. We spent a long time taking in our surroundings, without speaking. What was there to say? We both felt blessed to be looked after, and wanted it to last. We both knew it couldn't.

Astou returned a moment later with a plain white robe for Xavier, and a small chair. She sat the chair in the shade, and indicated that it was meant for me. She pointed to my fairer skin then at the sun. I was glad to get out of the sharp rays which were already setting me on fire. She handed the robe to Xavier who was determined to put it on himself. She had been about to do it for him, but even she could tell he'd reached his limit of being nursed. She secretly helped him out when she thought he wouldn't notice.

Xavier stood up to smooth out the fabric. The robe fell down over his long legs. The natural white of the cotton showed off his tanned olive skin. Astou and I both marvelled at how good he looked. Our ooohs and aaaaahs were echoed by the curious women in the neighbouring yards. The kids ran back in now, grabbing handfuls of white tunic, this time ignoring Astou's warnings. Xavier played with the kids before Astou shooed them away in an effort to preserve his ribs.

Xavier—despite the obvious pain it caused him—dragged the bench over by my chair in the shade so we could sit together. We watched Astou put a handful of tea leaves into a large earthenware pot and add water from a family-sized plastic jug. She then put the pot on a wrought iron rack that sat to one side of the fire pit. She fed the flames a little with some nearby brush and readied some small clay mugs around a makeshift table at our feet. She busied herself inside a moment and before we knew it she was frying up delicious-looking fritters on the open flames.

The smoke wafted over in our direction. The fritters smelled so good my stomach growled. Xavier laughed at me and stroked my complaining stomach with his good hand.

"Aren't you hungry?" I asked, expecting more empathy than sympathy.

"I am, but I am more worried that we are staying here too long," he admitted. "It is good that we will eat—but we should eat fast. We need to keep moving. I would like to get you to a safe place. And I would like to visit a hospital."

We didn't have to wait long before Astou was feeding us the hot fritters and tea. We thanked her but were so ravenous we said nothing further while we sated our hunger. The fritters were delicious, crispy clumps of some kind of bean paste, mixed with onions and other vegetables that I didn't immediately recognize.

We communicated our appreciation as best we could. Xavier attempted a few phrases in French but Astou's grasp of the language was worse than mine. I tried gesturing about how good the food tasted, and that seemed to go over well. Xavier was fidgeting and by the time our tea was low kept glancing at the house. I knew how he felt—I half expected gun-toting heavies to break through the back door any moment.

Astou picked up on our anxiety, but shrugged it off.

"Il reviens, il reviens," she assured us as she cleaned up. I offered to help but she waved me off.

Xav began to pace, a small cloud of dust building up at his feet. I took his hand and coaxed him back to the shade of the bench.

"We must go," he insisted, but gave in.

"I know. But do we even know where we are? How far are we from Dakar? How many hours to the next town, even? I'm sure it's not safe to travel at night. Even with you."

This last comment made him smile, and he squeezed my hand. His eyes, however, were glued to the back door of the concrete block house, awaiting the return of Amadou, or something much worse.

But Amadou arrived, free of henchmen. He and Astou had a long conversation in their own language. It started matter-of-factly, peppered with mirth, but concluded on a very serious note. Astou nodded and disappeared into the house.

Amadou grabbed himself a fritter from the table, and sat down across from us in another chair. He pulled a crinkled piece of paper from the pocket of his shorts. There were a few scribbled names on it, with arrows, followed by a note in a different language. The names turned out to be villages between here and a town about five hours away. The note was for us to give to

Amadou's cousin, who lived there. It contained explicit instructions for him in our regard.

Amadou also had money for us.

Xavier was grateful for the financial offer, but turned it down. Amadou shook his head, and explained, I assumed, why we would need money or why he felt giving us money was the right thing to do. Xavier accepted it in the end, after insisting on a proper address for Amadou in order to repay him once we were safely home. Amadou agreed to the concession.

Xavier stood, ready to go, but Amadou spread his palm in a gesture of patience. He turned to the door, waiting for good news. As the seconds passed, I watched his hand lower slowly behind him until eventually it brushed the edge of his leg. His shoulders fell, too, and he gave up on his surprise.

Amadou led us through his small house and back to the dirt road with its stick fencing. The sun beat down hard on us without the shelter of the courtyard trees. We turned left, moving away from the water and more deeply into the small fishing village. Xavier's burdening limp slowed our progress. The hot dirt under our feet bordered on painful. I wondered how safe we were to be walking barefoot, or walking slowly. There was not much that could be done about either.

The road drew a wide curve at the end of the line of concrete shops and houses. The buildings were further spread out here, and were typically smaller and hidden back from the road by deeper brush. A noisy machine shop with an entire yard full of boat motors and unidentifiable parts marked the end of the stick fencing. Up ahead, a small group of people gathered at what appeared to be an intersection with an actual paved road.

A cry went up behind us.

Xavier jumped and turned, ready to take on whatever was coming at us.

But it was only Astou—animated despite an armload of items—chasing after us with her high-pitched shouts.

She arrived breathless, ignoring the disapproving glare of her father. She handed Xavier a large bottle of water which he took with his one good hand, and me a small package wrapped in bright cloth. She shook Xavier's splinted hand with enthusiasm, cradling it in her excited one. She turned to me and shook both my hands as they cradled the wrapped package. She stood back and examined me, frowning. She undid the cloth at my waist and before I knew what was happening had retied it loosely around my head and shoulders. She nodded at Xavier for approval. His eyes shone back at her, so I must not have looked too odd. I received a warm embrace from her, her gift bundle squishing between us. She said something briskly to her father, and turned away from us back up the road of shops.

Amadou watched her leave and then shook our hands as well. He had a short conversation with Xavier about where we were going, and where to stop if it got dark before then. Then he was on his way.

The other people waiting for the bus stared at us intently. I stared back at them—it was only fair. All of them had shoes. Where did they get them? I had seen no shoes in the shops along the road. I looked down at my bare feet, so pale against the dry red dirt. The patches of blue and purple and brown appearing on my legs were going to get deeper over the course of the day. Xavier's were worse, but at least his darker skin made for a less dramatic contrast.

There were five other people waiting with us: a single man, a lone woman, and a couple with a small child. The family were dressed in traditional robes, including the boy, which was unlike the dress of the other children back at Amadou and Astou's house. They carried a few small wrapped parcels with them, and a stuffed plaid plastic suitcase. The woman's hair was braided up above her head beautifully, and a pair of bead earrings hung down, grazing her shoulders. The man wore a small cap on the top of his head, an elaborate design stitched along the rim. He stood between us and his wife and son, his back turned to them. The boy's face appeared occasionally from behind his father's robe, huge brown eyes staring up at me or at Xav. Whenever I caught the boy's glance I would smile at him, but his eyes would grow wider and he would disappear behind the robe.

The single man wore a t-shirt that said "Fightin' Irish" on

it, with a big graphic of the Boston Celtic's leprechaun character. The shirt was well worn, and his dark skin showed through in more than a few places, more obvious against the whiteness of the shirt. It was clean though, which couldn't be said for his shorts. They were covered in what looked like grease stains. He saw me looking at them and took a few steps toward me before Xavier put himself between us, making me an offer of Astou's water. I wasn't sure if he had noticed the other man approaching or not, but was glad when the stranger changed his mind about coming over.

The other woman had paid us little attention after her first examination. She was traditionally dressed as well, although less formally so. Her head was wrapped up in a bright-patterned cotton that matched that of her loose dress. She carried a chicken under her arm, and a tied burlap sack at her feet.

Xavier and I seemed to be the only ones in the bunch who bothered looking up and down the road for any sign of vehicle. There was some shade here, but not much. The hot sun creeping to its zenith burnt through the thin leaf cover of the few scrawny trees. No one spoke much. The sounds of the village behind us travelled down the dirt road, blocking out any bird sounds from the scattered trees of the intersection. The "Fightin' Irish" man had moved a little away from the rest to sit on a solid crate at the side of the other road. I envied his rest.

Our fellow travellers suddenly animated. I didn't see anything but they were all picking up their various goods. I listened but could only hear the sounds of the machine shop halfway down the road. However, moments later a white mini-van came careening around a far corner. The van was plastered with stickers and painted with stars and happy sayings in all variety of colours. It stopped in front of us and let off an elderly couple with a young girl about ten years old. Everyone shook hands together accompanied by big grins and excited conversation until the impatient driver of the van began honking his horn. A younger man helped people stuff their luggage through the open side door of the already crowded van. He took fare as the new passengers climbed through into the dark interior.

Xavier had his little piece of paper out, and approached the driver. The ticket taker eyed us while he stuffed his passengers into the van. The driver didn't understand what Xav was asking, but it was evident that the towns written on our piece of paper were not where he was going. The ticket-taker interrupted their broken conversation, and told Xavier, in French, that another ride would come by going the way we wanted.

"Soon?" Xavier asked, squinting up at the hot sun.

"Oui, bien sur," replied the young man, before slapping the roof of the van and holding on tight as it lurched forward, still hanging half in half out of the open sliding door.

We were alone.

Xavier paced, reviving the dust cloud of before.

"Do you always pace like this?" I asked, trying to make light of the situation.

He grunted, and kept pacing, but glanced at me sideways while doing so.

"It's just… the dust," I complained, trying to wave it out of the air as it rose around us.

He laughed and wrapped his generous arms around me, burying his face into my neck. His growing whiskers tickled and I squeezed away, giggling. He held onto my shoulders, turning us so the sun was behind him, hoping that his shadow could block out some of the sun for me. It couldn't—the sun was now high above us, our shadows virtually invisible in the dust beneath us.

"That's the second time Astou's bundle has been squished!" I laughed at the awkward lump between us.

It was as good a time as any to see what was inside. I undid the twine at the top, making a cradle between my left arm and my chin. She'd packed us some of the fritters, a couple of bananas, and a whole bunch of aloe leaves.

"Those are for you, I think," observed Xav, pointing at the aloe, impressed by Astou's thoughtfulness.

But there was another lump in the cloth underneath the food. I folded back the fabric to reveal two pairs of worn flip-flops, one small, one big. I immediately picked them out and dropped them on the ground. I wrapped the bundle back up, happy for the aloe which I would definitely need by the end of the day. Xavier slipped his bruised feet into the big pair of flip-flops, and laid out the smaller pair for me.

"Do you think these are theirs?" I wondered as I slipped my toes under the plastic bridge.

"I think so," chuckled Xavier, whose feet hung over both ends of his pair.

I had to agree, looking down at my own feet surrounded by a wide field of spare rubber sole.

We laughed together, and waited for our ride.

Chapter 10

Xavier and I spoke about the hospitality we'd been so lucky to find. We weighed the possibilities of the freighter crew figuring out our exact landing location. We changed the subject.

And we waited.

Xavier paced.

The sun lowered enough that Xavier was able to provide enough shade. I couldn't complain about having to stand so close to him to receive it.

Finally, a big flatbed truck rumbled around the corner from the same direction the mini-van had gone. It rolled to a painful stop, jerking to rest just as I wondered whether we should be sticking our thumbs out or something. The truck bed had a low perimeter wall which contained the few passengers sitting on a centre bench, surrounded by their sacks of goods. They peered over the side of the truck at us, curious.

Xavier asked the two men in the truck cab about the town names on our precious slip of paper. The ticket-taker in the passenger seat turned to say something to the driver, and then waved us with little interest to the back of the truck.

I put a foot up on the bumper, and someone from inside the flatbed reached down to give me a hand. I grasped it, and was lifted without effort to perch on the rear wall. The passengers in the truck sat back-to-back on the benches running down the centre of the flatbed. The men and women moved over a little to give us room to sit. I stepped over the tailgate into the back, having to inch my robe up in order to do so. While I was relieved to finally be putting some space between us and our pursuers, I still found time to worry about whether anyone was staring at my pale bare legs.

Xavier climbed in right behind me, but was having some difficulty manoeuvring over the tailgate. The other passengers howled with laughter as he lifted his long robe up over his knees to get clear of the raised tailgate. They had no idea what bad shape his ribs or his leg were in. He took the ridicule with a grin, and finally made it into the seat beside me just as the truck jerked forward onto the road.

The truck's benches were hard and unforgiving, making it a blessing that the main road here was paved, even if roughly so. Xavier took my hand and held it in his, hidden under the folds of our robes. I leaned my head against his shoulder but the ride proved too rough to keep it there.

The truck dropped most of the passengers off at the next fishing village, before the road turned away from the sea. We didn't have much to add to the minimal chatter of the few remaining passengers. I was glad for the cloth around my head which helped hugely in keeping the harsh rays off my face. The sun was casting longer shadows now. It wouldn't be too long before the light was gone, and we were travelling in an unsafe darkness. At least we had shoes.

We passed another dirt road intersection and let all but two other people off the truck. The man who rode with the driver in the cab opened his door and climbed into the flatbed from the front. He said something in local dialect to everyone in general. The two other passengers nodded and spoke agreement. Xavier asked for a French translation, but the man just shrugged his shoulders, not comprehending. He got back in the cab and we continued on.

I opened our little parcel and offered Xav a fritter. He was happy to have it. I wrapped the rest back up after helping myself to one, too. It was better to save what was left, given the waning light.

We watched the sun set with a mix of awe and apprehension. The landscape around us was a never-ending parade of shrubby trees and dry soil. Once in a while, a dirt path or rutted tire tracks would cut across our own at an odd angle, hinting at other life. But mostly, the view was one of dust and clumps of small trees disappearing into the distance.

As the darkness eclipsed us, a few shapes of buildings popped up against the violet sky. The gaps between the buildings shrank until it was apparent we were now on the main street of a small village. There were few lights—most were coming from small lanterns or backyard cooking fires.

The truck stopped.

The last two passengers disembarked, taking the rest of the burlap and cloth bundles with them. The truck driver and his cab partner looked at us through the opening of what had once been a glass window in the back of the cab. They were waiting for us to get out of the truck.

"Kaolack?" asked Xavier, indicating the town. Kaolack was where we were hoping to end up.

"Demain," replied the driver, after he and his partner had stopped laughing.

"Est-ce qu'il y a un hôtel ou nous pouvons rester?" asked Xavier with enthusiasm after hearing his own language.

It was too much French too fast, and was returned with blank stares.

"Hôtel?" Xavier repeated slowly, miming his head down on a pillow of his own hands.

The two men shrugged in the same way they had steered us to the back of their truck. I guessed they knew of a place like a hotel, but not a hotel like what I imagined a hotel to be.

I couldn't have been more correct.

The truck rolled ahead about fifty feet before slamming to a stop at the edge of the road.

The men got out of the cab and waved at us to follow them across the road. I climbed over the back of the tailgate pretty much the same way I had climbed in. Xavier, however, balanced himself against one side wall and gracefully swung both legs over before jumping to the ground. He had apparently been studying the exit method of the other passengers climbing out in their long robes. His landing, however, was as artless as a burlap sack. His one leg wasn't strong enough to take his full weight, and he fell down on all fours with a groan.

96

Xavier didn't stay on the ground long, and was at the rear bumper in time to give me a hand. The two men shook their heads. Crazy foreigners. I slapped at a mosquito. It would be the first of many.

The single story concrete block "hotel" sat back from the road behind a row of low gangly shrubs. A dirt yard filled the space between. A single flickering light bulb that hung freely over the front door implied that at least the hotel operated a generator. A cracked concrete slab step led up to the carved wooden door. Someone had painted a bright coloured sign on the wall above at some point, but the name had worn to the point of illegibility.

Inside we found a simple, unadorned concrete foyer. Two hallways ran off of it in opposite directions. At the back of the foyer, under another hanging light bulb, a ramshackle table stood in as a reception desk. A man sat napping behind it, his head resting on the spiral-bound registration notebook. A grid was painted on the wall behind the table. Rusty keys hung from nails hammered into each square of the grid. Beside each nail was a faded painted number, which I assumed corresponded to the room numbers.

The driver and his passenger woke the concierge and arranged a room for themselves before coordinating a second room on our behalf. The concierge asked to be paid in advance. Xavier must have been familiar with the Senegalese currency, as he knew exactly which bills to pull from the small wad Amadou had given us. The concierge didn't offer any change.

The sleepy concierge grabbed two keys off the nails behind him, and moved past us into the left hallway without a word. This time we all shrugged. As a group we followed the man down the dimly lit concrete corridor. The room doors were spread out down the left side of the corridor, their numbers completely illegible. The doors were built of dark carved wood—a stark contrast to the blank concrete walls. There were only a couple of doors on the opposite wall. One of them stood open to the exterior, letting the sounds of crickets waft in.

The first room the concierge unlocked was near the foyer. He flipped a switch inside the door and another bare bulb flickered to life. This one wasn't a hanging bulb, but a rusting sconce barely balanced against the near wall. Two single wooden beds were visible inside, each with a thin foam pad. That was it. The concierge handed the key to the truck driver, and moved on. The two men nodded goodnight to us, the driver confirming with hand signals that they would leave early in the morning, and would knock on our door. They shut their door behind them.

We turned to follow the concierge only to find him already halfway down the hall. We chased after him, our flip-flops echoing against the flat walls. He pointed at a door on our right, and used the local word, but the fading man and woman symbols were visible enough. The symbols shared the same door.

He stopped at another door on the left a few feet beyond. The door was dark wood, like the others, and had a faded number I couldn't make out any more than the name of the hotel. I guess as long as the key fit . . . The concierge unlocked the door to reveal another bare room with just one single bed, lit by another bare bulb in a rusty sconce. I was sure I saw something scurry into a crack in the far corner of the room. The bed sat in the middle of the room, slightly askew. Above it a hook stuck out of the stained ceiling at a funny angle—for a mosquito net.

Xavier noticed me looking at it. He got the attention of the concierge, pointing up at the hook while shrugging his shoulders in a question. The concierge shook his head, glancing back at Xav on his way out of the room like he was out of his mind. He left the door open behind him. I shut it and was tempted to lean against it but when faced with the room was reminded of why that might be a bad idea.

Once we were alone, I felt the knot of fear creep down the back of my neck and return to the pit of my stomach. We were leaving a trail of people who could easily identify us. It wouldn't be that hard to figure out the general area we had landed, knowing the time we had escaped and the position of the freighter, especially if that other body nearby came from the same ship. How long would we have before the shelter of strangers failed to protect us?

I wrapped my arms around Xavier's waist to distract

myself.

"I am so glad to finally be alone with you," I said.

"I am sorry this room is so… how do you say… rough?" he lamented.

"It's ok."

It may have been made of barren and stained concrete, lit drastically by a rusted sconce, and entirely void of any bedding, but it was better than what we'd been through.

"Ouch," he warned, when I squeezed him too hard.

He loosened my arms and enclosed me in his own.

"You must be exhausted," he murmured into my hair.

"I guess," I agreed. "But I think I'm too scared to sleep."

A mosquito landed on his arm by my face. I killed it with a quick slap.

He sighed.

"We will be ok," he assured me. "We will be at Amadou's cousin's house before noon tomorrow. No one will find us there. We will walk to the house from the place that the truck stops so that only we know where we have gone. We will drive directly to Dakar—there will be enough time left in the day to arrive there safely before nightfall."

"What if the cousin isn't there?"

"He will be there."

He pulled away to look at me. I could see my scared reflection in his sympathetic eyes. If he was so resolved to be strong, then I would be too. It was only fair.

"What about Amadou and Astou?" I asked. "If the Scar tracks them down…"

Xavier flinched and turned away. I would learn much later how deep a nerve my question struck. He took a deep breath with his back to me, and coughed when that aggravated his ribs. He sank down on the edge of the bed.

"I think that Amadou and Astou will be ok also," he responded at last, looking up at me. I got the sense that he meant to convince himself as much as me. "There are too many villages."

"But that body… "

"If he looks for us on the coast, we will not be there. He

knows we must go to Dakar. He will be waiting for us there."

"Oh…," I sagged. Something to look forward to.

I scratched the bites on my arm.

"I think that we must sleep with our clothes on," observed Xavier as he reached for the cloth package at the end of the bed. He found one of the pieces of aloe and squeezed the broken end. The thick translucent sap oozed out onto his fingers. He spread the aloe on my arm where the bites congregated. It was cool to the touch, and instantly soothing.

"Thank you," I sighed.

He put more where my skin had burnt, and where the welts tracked across my back. I dabbed some on the cut on his face. The stitches were hideous.

"Is it that bad?" asked Xavier when he caught my grimace.

"When it heals you will have a fabulously handsome scar," I assured him. My stomach gurgled. "Are there any fritters left?"

"There are two bananas."

"I guess we should split one now, and have the other for breakfast?"

"You have it. I do not need any."

"No way," I refused, and divided it. "You have to eat."

He feigned disinterest but accepted his ration anyway. It disappeared before I'd even taken a bite of my own.

"I just wish," I added through a mouthful, "that I had my toothbrush."

"Your toothbrush! That never leaves your side! But, don't worry… someone will find *Orion* and you will get your toothbrush back."

"They might find the pieces."

"The pieces?"

"Oh…" My chewing slowed to a stop.

He didn't know about the explosion.

"What do you mean 'pieces'?"

He asked in a tone that implied he already knew the answer was something he didn't want to hear. I didn't want to say it out loud and make it real, but there was no choice. It had happened— the boat was gone. I managed somehow to tell him what they had

100

done to *Orion*. He had meant to offer me sympathy for losing one of the few objects I had retained from my uncle's boat, but the weight of the loss of his own yacht sank his heart. He lay back on the bed in despair. The bed was so small he completely filled it.

"You would have been killed," he stammered through closed eyes. I had been avoiding that line of thought.

"But I wasn't. So we should try and get some sleep," I advised.

I stretched myself out on top of him. He rested his arms around my back, nuzzling the top of my head where it rested against him. I felt great comfort in having him so close.

It was short-lived, however, as my weight was too painful for his ribs to carry.

"Can you lie on your side?" I asked, hoping.

"Peut-être," he responded, turning himself to the left. After a brief wince, he responded, "Oui, je peux faire ca."

"Then we can spoon," I declared with delight.

"Spoon?" He asked as I squeezed myself against him along the edge of the bed.

"Spoon," I explained, as we adjusted ourselves against each other within the confines of the narrow bed.

"Spoo...," he repeated in appreciation, but had fallen asleep before he finished the word.

***

I woke up a short time later having to pee. The light was still on. Xavier was rasping in my ear, and the unhealthy sound of it unnerved me. But, first things first. I had a sandal already on one foot, and found the other on the floor. I glanced around for any large creepy crawlies before slipping it on. I coaxed a sleeping Xavier onto his back, knowing he would be more comfortable that way. I'd figure out where I'd fit when I came back.

I didn't know what Xavier had done with the room key, but I was willing to risk the remote chance of intrusion to let him sleep.

The few hanging lights were still on in the hallway. I don't know what I would have done if they were not, as we had nothing along the lines of a flashlight or candles. The hard bare walls spit back the soft rubber thwacking of my sandals, disturbing the otherwise brooding quiet. The clack of the bathroom door's cheap hardware echoed down the corridor and back, announcing my visit to anyone who may have been awake.

I almost changed my mind once I saw the inside of the shared bathroom, but I didn't really have much of a choice. By the dim light from the hallway I found a switch for yet another bare bulb housed in a sconce more rusty—if that was possible—than the room fixtures. The bathroom was bare except for a single toilet which lacked a seat. A bucket of water with a small plastic pitcher resting beside it indicated the toilet was not hooked up to running water, either. I guessed that was why no one had bothered installing a sink. So for many reasons, the room stank of urine.

I locked the door behind me by its small hook latch. I hiked my borrowed robe up high enough that I could squat over the toilet bowl without touching anything. I noted with some relief that the toilet itself was fairly clean. I had to drip dry, there being no toilet paper in sight, and by the time I thought it was safe to stand upright without the cover of underwear, my legs burnt from the strain.

Back in the room, Xavier was sound asleep, still on his back. I pushed his good leg over to one side so that I could sleep inverse to him. I hugged his legs for whatever security that gave me, and hoped their weight might prevent me from slipping off the edge of the bed during the night. I heard my stomach growl as I drifted off.

I slept for only a moment before a sharp rapping on the door startled us awake. Xavier winced after sitting bolt upright in response to the noise. He looked at me clinging to his legs at the opposite end of the bed and started to laugh.

"How did you get there?" he asked. My sleepy response was interrupted by a muffled shout through the door.

"Nous partons!"

"Nous venons!" Xavier shouted back.

We were dressed, apart from the scarf I'd had around my

head the day before. I had no idea how Astou had tied it, and as there was no mirror, I wrapped it around my waist—at least for now, until the sun started to creep up in the sky. For the moment, from what I could tell, it was still dark outside.

We were out the door fast, but found ourselves chasing after the drivers who were already starting up the truck across the street. Xavier limped ahead of me. I was worried about losing the oversized flip-flops while running.

The driver gunned the motor, impatient, as the two of us stumbled over the tailgate into the back of the truck. We knew to sit right up behind the cab this morning so that we might get some shade from it for the first part of the day. We grabbed at the bench under our legs when the truck lurched forward into the town.

The purple of the early sky paled, giving the buildings lining the street some definition beyond the silhouettes of the night before. The town was a bigger place than the coastal village we had come from, but not much. Figures were stirring at the backs of a few of the shops and houses. Most were women who were rising to start the breakfast fires or to sweep the yard while the tea brewed.

As we rolled along the main street I surmised that we had driven through the "busy" part of town already. More of the buildings were houses than shops, sparser and smaller than the ones we'd seen on arriving. The shops that were operating seemed more make-shift, as if the people running them had found no place to sell their wares and so had thrown a few scraps together and called the place a store. We stopped at a point on the edge of town where the trees were more numerous than the scattered dwellings.

I peeked over the edge of the truck siding to see why we'd stopped but it was unnecessary. A small crowd of travellers were already throwing their sacks of goods into the truck. They followed their belongings with the same elegant grace that Xavier had tried to emulate the night before. Every single one of them stopped mid-climb, just for a split second, when spotting us in the truck. Once they'd registered our paler presence they would continue as if nothing were out of the ordinary.

Most people in the back of the truck did not speak French

but Xavier struck up a conversation with a teenage boy who was on his way to Dakar for school. The boy had cousins there, but neither family had a car so he was on his own in getting to the city. It was faster from here to take the inland route to Dakar rather than to travel back along the coast. Through Xavier's new friend we were introduced to a woman who knew the house we were seeking in the next town. We had a guide to our destination now, but had lost our anonymity.

The ride was—apart from the distraction of conversation—pretty much what it had been the previous day. The land was drier than it had been on the coast, and so the trees were slightly smaller and farther apart. They scattered into the distance across a dry, barren land covered in sparse grass and thorny-looking shrubs. The cloud of dust behind us had grown big enough to swallow some of the truck itself. It wasn't long before I untied my scarf from my waist and put it around my head—the sun hadn't even risen over the shelter of the truck cab.

I was ravenous after a couple of bumpy hours, and salivating for the last half of a banana. I unwrapped the package from Astou. I tried sucking on one of the broken leaf ends of the aloe, but the sap was bitter. I was disappointed.

I noticed the whiteness of Xavier's knuckles as he clung to the edge of the wooden bench. The bumps must have been seriously painful for his broken ribs. His face betrayed none of the pain his fingers did, relaxed as he was in easy conversation with fellow passengers. I hoped for his sake that we would arrive sooner rather than later.

Chapter 11

The air was hotter here than it had been on the coast. Everyone in the back of the truck was noticeably sweating—it wasn't just us this time. Sweat stains grew on all the men's clothing, suggesting an additional reason for the more common white robe colour.

We came to the next town as the sun reached its highest point in the sky. The other passengers became more animated, adjusting their goods and their clothes, and looking around more aggressively. The ride smoothed out as the dirt gave way to actual pavement, shops and fencing appeared along the thin line of a cross-road as it bent in the distance. The town announced itself in the same manner as the previous towns had, with scattered shanty shacks and the beginning of stick fencing. The shacks we passed grew bigger and denser, the shops housed in more permanent structures. We saw people carrying their loads in carts or on bicycles rather than on their heads. We were honked at by other vehicles. But it wasn't until I saw a two-story building that I knew this town was much, much, bigger than the ones we had experienced so far.

We stopped at an intersection. The woman who had offered to guide us to our next shelter urged the young student to get the attention of the driver through the cab window.

The truck pulled over with an abrupt stop.

"I think that we have arrived," whispered Xavier, releasing his death grip from the wooden bench. The woman disembarked ahead of us, and Xavier passed her belongings to her. He told me to go ahead while he said goodbye to the young man. There was much hand-shaking. By the time I had manoeuvred myself off the truck, he had caught up with me. I wasn't fooled by his easy manner this time. I could tell he was covering immense pain.

The truck driver honked twice as he drove on away from us. A dozen dark faces fixed their curiosity on us until the truck turned a corner a few blocks ahead. By that point we had followed our guide into a laneway hidden between two non-distinct buildings.

The lane was nothing more than a dirt track bordered on either side by solid walls or huge wooden gates. Whatever lay behind the walls remained a mystery. Some of the gates bore smaller inset doors, but they, too, were solid. Dogs barked behind a few of them as we strolled by. Once, a Landrover exited through a gate ahead of us. The driver gave us a quick once-over before driving on in the opposite direction. The face of the driver was white—a very tanned white, but definitely white. A dark robed figure shut the gate behind the vehicle and no hint of the world within was visible by the time we passed it.

An intersection with a busy street lay ahead, and beyond that our scenery would change. The enclosed lane was coming to an end. I was sorry I wouldn't get a chance to peek inside the high walls around us to uncover their secrets.

But before we reached the end our guide pointed to one of the more discreet doors on her left and stopped walking. A small intercom was mounted on the wall next to the door, and a motion-detector security light mounted above it. No names or numbers were written on the wall around the door nor on the door itself. The large driveway gate was equally blank. Xavier showed her the paper again, to be sure. She nodded and smiled encouragement. Then after much hand shaking, she continued on her way to a gate at the end of the row.

I reached to press the intercom buzzer but Xavier intercepted my outstretched finger.

"I have been thinking…" he started.

"You think this is a bad idea…?"

"No," he smiled through his pain. "About *Orion*'s explosion. I am thinking that it would be better if it was an accident."

"Well, ya…," I said, not catching his meaning.

"I am thinking that it would be safer if we *say* that it was an accident."

"Oh. I don't understand. Safer?"

"When we arrive in Dakar—today, I hope—we will have to explain to our embassies how it is that we arrived here with no passports and no money…"

Right. I'd been delaying dealing with that, but I'd just planned to tell the truth.

"I am thinking it would be safer for us if we do not bring attention to ourselves with stories of pirates. Or kidnapping. The news would not stay quiet. They would know how to find us."

"Isn't that why we report it? So the police can catch them and we don't have to run anymore?"

"I have tried that but the police…"

"—are incompetent. And corrupt. So you've said." His distrust of the police was partly responsible for our perilous situation and my annoyance at the heat of the sun and this alley of blind gates made my distaste of his opinion worse.

"I will try to explain that," he sighed, gathering his patience. "Imagine that you must try to help a blind man destroy a hornet's nest, but you can only tell him where to swing at it with his stick. He will hit the nest, maybe, but the hornets escape and are too small, too fast, and too many to destroy before they attack the man."

"If the blind man had the right tools? A really big stick and some smoke…" I hypothesized, but could picture the futility of the scene.

"It does not work. The blind man is defeated and the hornets, they build a new nest."

"So they get away with everything they did? And we have to lie about what happened and stay hidden like we were the criminals?"

"They will not get away with it. We will report what happened to someone I trust. But until then, yes, we must hide."

"So we will tell someone eventually?"

"Yes. I promise."

"And what do we say in the meantime?" I was dubious.

"Propane," suggested Xavier, and shrugged a shoulder.

He buzzed the non-descript beige intercom.

A static-laden voice came back in dialect I now understood to mean, "Yes?"

Xavier answered in slow, clear French that we were sent by Amadou and were here to see Abdoulaye. He added that we had a message for him. Voiceless static came back in reply, followed by silence. We looked at each other with apprehension. If this didn't work out, we'd be on our own looking for a place to stay with little money to pay for anything.

My thoughts were interrupted by the sound of the latch on the other side of the small gate. It creaked open to reveal a dark and wary man who examined us up and down.

"Abdoulaye?" asked Xavier, fingering Amadou's note.

The man shrugged, but it was unclear whether the shrug was an acknowledgment or a guarded greeting.

"J'ai une petite note pour lui…," began Xavier, handing over the written message Amadou had laid out for his cousin before we left.

The man took it politely. He unfolded it and as he gave it a brisk read, the lines in his forehead increased. He scrutinized us further then shrugged, tucking the note in a pocket of his robe.

"Je m'appelle Abdoulaye," he introduced himself finally, shaking our hands in turn. "Entrez."

He stepped back and held the gate open for us to walk through.

The entry opened up into a world that took my breath away. The high walls around the garden blocked out the busy street noises that flooded through the laneway from both ends. The path from the gate wound to a very modern looking home at the end of the long drive. There were no cars in the driveway but the garage, just visible around the far corner of the low wide house, could have held three cars behind its closed doors. Luscious bright flowers of all shapes and sizes—mostly large—filled the yard. A broad wooden roof and thick wood columns sheltered the low stone porch at the entrance to the house.

Xavier and Amadou's cousin conferred ahead of me as they fell into a slow stroll together. I could tell from the cautious tone in Abdoulaye's voice that he was unsure about us. I sympathized to an extent. We were clearly foreigners, but didn't have the typical appearance of tourists—not even of backpackers who travelled on the lowest budgets. I knew both Xavier and I showed evidence of recent violence, and neither of us was as clean as we should have been. Our clothes fit poorly and made no sense. We were extremely lucky that Abdoulaye's affection for (or obligation to) his cousin outweighed the potential risk we posed.

Xavier turned to wait for me when we reached the front veranda.

"This is a beautiful place," I said, taking his outstretched hand.

"We are lucky the owners are away. I am told that Abdoulaye would not be able to help us if the owners were at home," Xavier rasped. I noticed the beads of sweat on his face from the heat weren't drying here the way they had in the sun. He looked around with equal admiration at the warm modern design visible from the vestibule. He moved slowly.

Inside we were treated a smartly-designed open-concept home nestled under a wide low roof with open rafters. Heavy wooden beams cut across the ceiling space just above the soft white walls. Broad sliding glass doors ran most of the length of the living space towards the yard. The polished stone floor of the living room continued outside to the patio, enhancing the sense that the gardens were part of the living space. Large potted plants throughout the house added to the effect, while also serving to divide the vast space within. The architecture mastered a beautiful balance between cutting edge European design and traditional Senegalese motifs.

Abdoulaye indicated we should take a seat on the couch and wait for him to return.

Xavier sighed audibly as he sank into the soft brown leather. I plopped down beside him, closing my eyes as I rested my head back against the seat. It felt wonderful to sit on something pliant that didn't shake or bump.

"Abdoulaye will drive us into Dakar," Xavier filled me in on his earlier conversation. "He has some supplies he needs to collect. He has gone to tell his wife. They live in a small area at the back of the house. He is the groundskeeper; she does the cooking for the couple who live here."

"Who are the homeowners?"

"The husband manages a large bottling plant in the town, and the wife works at an NGO—he did not say which one. They are French, I think."

"And Abdoulaye and his wife live in the back?"

"Yes, that is what I was told."

"That seems unfair…"

"Yes, that is what I was told," Xavier humoured me.

I turned my head to get a better look at his expression. His eyes were closed, but he had a wide smile on his lips. His breathing had become very shallow, scarily so.

"You need to go to a hospital."

"Pas ici…"

I watched his smile fade.

"Are you in pain?" I asked.

He didn't answer.

"Xav?"

I nudged him a little and his head lolled to one side. I could see the ashen pallor of his skin now that the sun didn't brighten his face. I put my hand against his forehead and felt the dampness. He needed a doctor. Now. I saw a phone across the room and started towards it, not knowing who I would call once I got there.

Abdoulaye interrupted my panic when he returned to the room with his wife in tow. He introduced her as Fatima, and jangled his car keys at me. I shook my head and indicated my motionless sweetheart.

"Il dort?" Abdoulaye strode around the couch, ready to shake Xavier awake so we could all leave.

"No!" I said. I put my arms across Xavier to protect him. "No, he's hurt!"

Abdoulaye stepped back and looked at his wife with a

dumb expression. He asked her a question in another language, shrugging. He pointed at me, shook his head, and then started pacing back and forth across the stone floor.

"What wrong?" asked Fatima. Her English caught me off guard.

"I…"

"What wrong with him?"

"Oh… He can't breathe. I don't know… I don't know why." But I did know why. His rib was broken. Maybe more than one. And now he was going to die and I would be left alone stranded in the middle of Senegal until some scar-faced monster tracked me down and murdered me, too. I needed to keep my head together. For Xavier—and for myself.

"His ribs," I said. I ran my arm across my own. "Broken."

Fatima leaned over to Xavier and laid a ginger hand on his chest. She felt the bandage through his shirt.

"Doctor bandage?" she asked.

"No doctor," I answered. "Only bandage."

"No doctor." She scowled when she said it, giving me a look like his predicament was my fault. Like it was my idea not to see a doctor! She wiped more sweat from Xavier's pale forehead, shaking her head and giving me another dirty look.

Fatima headed for the telephone sitting nearby and picked up the receiver. Abdoublaye scooted up behind her and put his finger down on the plunger. She swatted his hand away. This began a heated conversation between them that went on for several minutes. I didn't understand anything they said but the finger-pointing at Xavier and I gave me a hint. Fatima dialed mid-conversation, leading to an argument broken every few seconds by Fatima putting her hand up and speaking into the phone. The argument continued while she waited for the person she was trying to reach to be found on the other end. The fight ended when Fatima grinned and focused fully on her phone call. Abdoulaye threw his hands up and disappeared through the archway into the rear of the house, his vocal complaints waning in the distance.

Fatima spoke on the phone several minutes. Long pauses broke her string of French, during which she nodded and glanced over at Xavier. She hung up the phone.

"No bandage!" She said, coming back to the couch. "Very bad. Make infection."

Together we lifted Xavier to a sitting position and pulled off his robe to get at the bandaged ribs beneath. I held Xavier against me like a baby, his shallow breath wheezing against my chest. Fatima worked at the knots Astou had tied so tightly to keep his ribs still. As the bandages loosened, Xavier's chest visibly expanded and he began to cough. Though still unconscious, he moaned in pain.

"No bandage," Fatima repeated. She gently wiped a tear off my cheek I didn't notice had fallen. "Aspirin ok. Rest good."

She fluffed a pillow at the end of the couch and helped me lay Xavier down on his side. She brought me a cool damp cloth to help sooth Xavier's fever, and a glass of water for me to drink. She laid a dry towel at his head. Even unconscious, his body coughed up the heavy phlegm that had been drowning his restricted lungs. But until he regained consciousness, there would be no painkillers for him. Fatima drew a chair up alongside the couch.

"Sit," she said. I did.

Abdoulaye emerged from his proverbial cave with a look of determination, and waved for me to come with him outside. I shook my head but he insisted. A pick-up truck with the engine running waited for us at the front of the house. He opened the passenger door for me.

"Allons-y," he said.

"Où?" I asked, wondering where he would expect me to go with him.

"Dakar," he said. I looked back at the house. Why would he think I would leave Xavier behind? I realized that Abdoulaye planned to leave whether I joined him or not. He didn't care what I did, or what happened to Xavier, as long as we didn't interfere with his business. He shut the passenger door while I stood by, and got into the driver's seat. We had a big problem if he drove to Dakar without us.

"S'il vous plait," I begged him through the open window. "Attend. Un jour. S'il vous plait."

He shook his head and put the truck in gear. I walked a few steps with Abdoulaye as he drove towards the opened gate, repeating my plea in English to his deaf ears. He picked up speed, leaving me well behind. The truck rounded the turn into the alley and disappeared beyond the high garden walls in a cloud of dry red dust.

Fatima came outside to find me crying in the driveway. She steered me back into the cool house.

"He will come back," she promised.

She took me with her through the archway to the back of the house. The archway led to a narrow hallway which stepped down a short level parallel to the main space of the house. She opened a door half way down that led to a simple bedroom.

"You sleep," she insisted, pointing at the bed. "And shower. I keep watch."

I didn't argue. I knew how exhausted and dirty I looked—a genuine reflection of how I felt. I crept across the covers of the comfortable bed to pass out on top of them.

I couldn't sleep with so much fear and anxiety running through my mind. But a shower would refresh me a little. I washed myself, then put my dirty clothes back on for lack of a better option. The light bouncing through the pale curtains hinted at a darkening sky. Had I slept without knowing it?

I retraced my steps back to the big living room to check on Xavier. He remained prone as I'd left him, eyes shut, head resting on the brightly patterned pillow. His breathing was much more relaxed and deep now, almost peaceful. He no longer coughed. I brushed the hair back from his face.

"He sleep now. I give him aspirin."

I jumped at the sound of Fatima's voice.

She beckoned me to follow her back through the archway. She led me back down the back corridor, past the little guest bedroom, to where the long hallway ended with a framed view out to the garden. The wide roof jutted out above the opening which focused the view of the landscaping on a small grotto at the far side of the garden. We turned right just before reaching the opening to arrive at the rear abode that was Abdoulaye and

Fatima's home within the house.

The same overhanging roof that sheltered the main house patio also covered a modest brick patio here. Across from the hallway, on the opposite side of the patio, another door opened back into a small adjoining house from which fragrant aromas spilled. Fatima indicated that I should make myself comfortable on the patio, and then disappeared into the other door. I squinted inside after her to satisfy my curiosity about how they lived. Their place seemed spacious and well-kept and maybe it wasn't so bad after all. I took a seat on one of the pretty wooden lawn chairs that furnished Fatima and Abdoulaye's patio.

A relaxing breeze swept in from a divide between the main house and Fatima's abode, and kept the patio fairly cool relative to the oppressive heat. I thought the heat might have subsided with the sun going down, but my confusion about the late time of day vanished when the sky opened up and a thick wall of rain dumped down all around us.

The volume of water roared down the slope of the roof, collecting in a downspout that ran through a channel beneath our feet and into the garden. They had engineered a beautifully simple irrigation system.

Fatima returned with a big pot of rice and bowls for each of us. Like my exhaustion, I was numb to how hungry I felt until offered food. I gobbled the tasty rice with the enthusiasm of a starved stranger. Fatima smiled as she caught my eye, both of us content at the cool air, the delicious flavours, and the new company. The pounding sound of the rain drowned out any chance for conversation but substituted as dinner music instead. She was thrilled to see me admiring Abdoulaye's hard work in the garden. It was impossible not to admire what he'd done—the mix of glorious scents and fantastic colours nearly overwhelmed the senses.

Once sated, I asked Fatima for something that Xavier could eat. She shook her head at the rice and instead brought me a bowl of warm broth on a tray for him. Back in the living room, she helped me coax him upright on the couch. He moaned in complaint.

"Xavier," I whispered. "I brought you some soup to eat."

His eyes fluttered open and lit up when he saw me. Still, the pain leaked through his face. He let me spoon feed him for a bit before taking over for himself. He winced every time he lifted the spoon to his lips. He was in no shape to travel to Dakar without a dedicated ride. Not like this.

"Is there more aspirin?" I asked Fatima. She grabbed some from the main house kitchen, along with a glass of water.

I watched Xavier shift uneasily in his seat, holding his ribs as still as possible as he returned the glass to Fatima with appreciation. She took all the dishes on the tray and returned to the back.

"Can you sleep some more?" I asked Xavier.

"Yes. Easy," he smiled.

I helped him lie down and sat with him while he drifted back to sleep. My thoughts meandered to what lay ahead for us. I didn't even want to go to Dakar. Dakar represented an unknown future of frightening possibilities: abduction, separation, death. I knew we couldn't stay in Koalack forever, but if I could buy Xavier some recuperation time in this comforting shelter, I could put off Dakar. At the same time, we couldn't stay here forever, and it looked like it was up to me to find us another way there. I decided a good night's sleep wouldn't hurt my ability to broach the subject with Fatima. In the morning I would ask her to help us find another way to the capitol—one that granted us a few more days in this temporary paradise.

I kissed Xavier good night and went back to the spare bedroom. As I drifted into a heavy sleep I thought I heard Abdoulaye's voice from the living room. Fatima had said he would be back, despite the fervour of his departure. If it was Abdoulaye, I hoped that he would be willing to wait for several days more and still be willing to drive us to Dakar at the end of it.

***

A hard rapping on the door snapped me awake. I didn't know where I was at first, thinking I was back at the concrete hotel. Or worse, in a dingy room on an ocean vessel. Had they found us? I heard my own sharp intake of breath in the otherwise quiet room. A gentle hand touched my arm.

"Nous sommes en sécurité," assured Xavier's comforting voice from the dark.

"Uh?" I asked. When had Xavier joined me in the guest room?

"Je m'excuse. We are safe," he laughed. "But we must drive to Dakar. Abdoulaye is anxious to leave. I told him last night that it would be ok to go this morning."

"You sound better..."

"A little, yes. The problem must have been my robe. When I woke up it was missing. I looked for it and found you instead, which was much better. Your dress is here."

I felt the cloth of my borrowed dress pressed against my hand. Xavier flicked on the lights while I pulled it over my head.

"We had to take it off to get at the bandages around your ribs," I explained. "Your lungs were filling up with fluid and basically drowning—"

"We?" Xavier interrupted. I blushed, which made him giggle. Then cough.

"Maybe you can help me to put it back on?" he said, handing me his robe. "Just you."

He winked and carefully put his arms out for me to dress him. I sighed.

Fatima walked slowly with Xavier and me out to where Abdoulaye waited in his pick-up. I thought for a minute we would have to endure another long journey in a bumpy cargo bed but Abdoulaye got out and held the passenger door open for us. We shook Fatima's hand in farewell and thanked her for her hospitality. I let Xavier climb carefully in ahead of me to sit between myself and Abdoulaye.

"Allons-y," I said once I was in my seat with the door shut. It was the only time I would ever see Abdoulaye smile.

We were all quiet during the long drive. I watched as the sun rose on a familiar shrubby landscape. Every so often we would hit a bump in the road and Xavier's grip on the seat would tighten, but he seemed alright otherwise. We stopped for a pee break and a quick meal of rice about two hours into the drive. Abdoulaye allowed no other interruptions for the remainder.

Our entry into Dakar followed a prolonged transition similar to the previous night's small town arrival. Here the transition happened on a much, much bigger scale. Minarets dotted the landscape, jutting into the hazy heat of a crowded city sky above the rest of the buildings. The tighter corners and hasty stops increased as we drove further into town, making our cramped truck cab quarters much less bearable. I sat tight against the passenger door to give Xavier's ribs as much space as possible. I worried the door might fall open at any moment, spitting me out onto the road.

We arrived at a point where we were surrounded by multiple-story buildings and multiple-vehicle traffic. It was another universe to the sparse arid landscape we'd ridden in most of the day. People were shouting to each other in the street, honking madly, making poor driving decisions. We braked without warning to avoid a pair of teenagers rushing across the middle lane. Abdoulaye pounded on the wheel, but his mind was elsewhere. He muttered to himself, checking street and the names of the bigger stores. He squawked suddenly and we turned sharply to the right, crossed three lanes of traffic, and squeezed through a gate into a landscaping yard. Paving stones stacked to chest height filled the yard, not leaving much room for a truck to park or load. The place looked like a yard-sized chess board.

Abdoulaye spoke a few words in French, leaning over to shake Xavier's hand, then mine, and exited the truck. Xavier sighed and relaxed.

"We are here," he said, eying a tall stone bishop in the corner.

"Where's here, exactly?"

"I don't know, but we have some money for a taxi. That is all that we need to know."

I climbed out of the truck, holding the door open so Xavier could slide his tall frame out behind me. He moved with great care, a long way from the adept bougainvillea-climbing sleuth I had imagined on the boat.

The busy noises around us stopped as all the yard workers turned to focus on the white couple getting out of the work truck. The pause lasted only a moment, and then everything went back to what it had been, leaving us wondering if we had only imagined it. We picked our way through the piles of paving stones and pale clay tiles to the gated entrance at the road. The noise and crowd on the street engulfed us as we left the shelter of the yard, but no one paid us any attention at all. It was a bit of a relief.

Xavier had no trouble flagging a cab and in French directed the driver to take us to the Canadian embassy.

Reality sank in like a cold bath.

No money no passport no i.d. no clothes no name. A strong hand took hold of mine as with unfocused eyes I watched the crowded street theatre pass by. We rode frozen that way for a good half hour before pulling up at a clean, concrete-supported gate. The Mounties standing next to the entrance gave the location away.

"Mounties," I mumbled to myself in an attempt to change the direction of my own thoughts to embarrassment at that national stereotype.

"You will be fine. Your embassy will help you. Tell them the name of the boat of your uncle and that he is anchored in Mindelo—it is a small town. He will have reported you missing by now, I think. You will be able to get your papers. It will be ok."

"Aren't you coming with me?"

"I have to go to my own Embassy," he responded as if it was a given we would split up.

"But…" I had no way to contact him if anything went wrong.

"I will be back here soon—two or three hours, maybe. I think you will still be here, probably? Wait for me, if you are early. Be sure that they have a secure place for you to stay. Just in case. But I will be here."

The sincerity came through in his voice, but that wouldn't help once I left the comfort of the cab. I looked around at the strange faces on the street, and the stone faces of the Mounties at the gate. This was where the smugglers were supposed to be waiting for us. They could be lurking anywhere.

118

TEMPT the OCEAN

"The taxi will not leave until you are safely inside," he assured me. "And you look very much Canadian. They will let you in."

I caught the driver's eye in the rear-view mirror. He seemed to agree with Xavier, even if he didn't understand the particular words being used. I took a long last look at Xavier before I opened the door of the cab. He was very pale, and holding his splinted hand against his still ribs. His bristled cheeks had grown close to beard status at this point. He rested his head on the back of the seat, looking towards me, his big deep blue eyes imploring me to be strong. I worried for his sake that the French wouldn't let him in at their end.

"Propane," I whispered.

His lips curled up in a wan smile.

I planted a quick kiss and scrambled out of the cab without looking back. I crossed the wide sidewalk to the guarded gate without anyone attacking, and the stone-faced Mounties stepped aside and even held the gate open for me. I looked back from inside the gate but the narrow glimpse of the street afforded no view of the taxi I trusted was watching. I followed a shaded walkway across a paved entry yard to a set of glass doors and let myself in to the air-conditioned world of Canadian bureaucracy.

Chapter 12

Despite many signs in both French and English, it was not immediately evident where I should go. Line-ups trickled out from a few places, but none of them were obviously marked. The immediate sense I felt was one of empty promise—a vast space with no leads. I asked around and eventually found myself sitting across a bare desk from a tired-looking man in a short-sleeved dress shirt. I had managed to fill him in on the whereabouts of my passport, and all the details I could think of to facilitate communication with Bill and Margaret in Cabo Verde. He was now on the phone to someone more senior than himself.

"Apparently we've been looking for you," said the man, hanging up the phone. He pulled a few of the desk drawers open and shut without engaging any of the contents. "There's a report that will need verification. Can you wait here a moment?"

He left me on my own in the tiny room for what felt like several hours, entertained only by the faint sound of birds coming through a window above my sight line. There wasn't anything on the walls for distraction. The embassy worker returned eventually, superior in tow, and was kind enough to bring me a Coke. The senior worker was an aide in the department, and not impressed with me at all.

"What made you think embarking on a boat with a stranger was a smart thing to do?"

"He's not a stranger," I declared in both Xavier's and my own defence.

"Oh?" the senior official paused, checking the notes of the shirt-guy. "I thought you said you had just met him?"

120

"I did, but…"

"And that was when?"

"Uh…" I counted the days on my fingers, and had to guess about the dark hours on the freighter. "Five days ago . . . "

The senior official tossed the paperwork on the desk and ran a hand through his hair.

"It was a very, very stupid thing to do," he said.

"It's not his fault the boat blew up," I cried.

"Maybe," admitted the official, sitting behind the scattered papers on the desk. He gathered them up into a neat pile and studied me as he let out a long breath.

"I'd like to get some corroboration from him," he added. "You said this man has gone to the French embassy? Gerry, could you…"

"—It might be the Swiss," I interrupted, rethinking my assumptions.

The senior official looked at me hard.

"He lives in Paris, but he was born in Switzerland," I shrugged. "He didn't say which one he was going to."

"Right," responded the official, shaking his head. "And his name is—?"

"Xavier."

"Xavier…" He was waiting for me to finish. "Xavier what?"

I had no idea what his last name was.

I had to wait another hour, during which I was offered a cheese sandwich from the embassy commissary. Later still, shirt-guy returned to tell me they needed the room, and sent me back to wait in the broad echoing entrance hall.

I spotted Xavier immediately, pacing. He was tapping some papers against his leg impatiently. They looked like airplane tickets. He was no longer wearing Amadou's white robe, but had changed to a pair of light pants and a t-shirt. He must have gone shopping. I wished that he had waited—I would have been so glad to have something clean to wear. He brightened when he saw me.

"How long have you been here?" I asked after a light embrace.

"Two hours, I think," he confessed, but dismissed it quickly. "Are you ready to go?"

"No," I laughed, surprised by the question.

"What is it you are waiting for—what are they doing?"

"I don't know, really."

I sat down. Xavier looked around to see whose attention to grab. I took his sleeve and pulled him down into the chair beside me.

"It takes time sometimes," I explained. He couldn't grasp my complacency.

"It's like British bureaucracy," I tried.

"Bfff," he sputtered, hanging his head. "That is no good."

We had just managed to get comfortable enough to weave our legs together when I spotted shirt-guy coming towards us from the far end of the hall. Busy figures passed in front of him in either direction as he approached. He slowed for a fraction when he saw I was not alone. The shift in pace was almost imperceptible.

"You are lucky," he stated to me when he was within earshot. He shot Xavier a disapproving glance before returning his attention to me. "We have your passport number confirmed. We will have to put together a temporary one for you. In the meantime, your family in Mindelo are arranging a flight for you from Dakar. They seem to feel responsible."

Another disapproving glance.

"We have no accommodation at the embassy, but we do arrange to put people up at the University when necessary. I have directions here for you, and some emergency funds which you'll need to sign for." He handed me an official-looking envelope with a slip of paper and a pen.

"How long will the passport take?" Xavier cut in with a very authoritative tone.

Shirt guy almost jumped, like he wasn't expecting the spectre to speak.

"About five days, is my guess. Ten at the most," answered shirt-guy, but directed his answer to me in an attempt to ignore what he felt was the root of the problem.

"Cinq jours!" Xavier jumped up out of his seat. Shirt-guy

had to step back to avoid a collision. He looked around nervously for security. Several conspicuous armed men were intently focused on us.

"Are you the one whose boat she was on?"

"Xav—it's ok," I got up as well, taking his arm to diffuse the tension.

"It's not ok," he argued. "I am flying to Paris in three hours."

In a whisper only I could hear, he added, "I am afraid for you."

My heart sank.

"I have to go," he apologized, backing away. He meant now. Shirt-guy's face erupted in a victorious gloat.

"But..."

"I need that you will promise to stay here."

"In Dakar?" I was incredulous.

"At the Embassy."

"But they close..."

"I have to go to make some arrangements."

I couldn't believe he was just going to leave after making such a fearful declaration about my safety. I sat back down, giving him a hard look. He held my stare.

"Promise me that you will wait here."

"The best thing to do," put in shirt-guy, "would be to get a taxi and go to the university."

"Promise," repeated Xavier.

I promised, being the fool that I was. He left quickly, without even a kiss.

"There's enough money for a taxi," floated the unwelcome voice of shirt-guy through my state of abandonment. "It's about a thirty minute ride from here. There's a letter enclosed that's to go to the office. They close at 6."

"I promised I'd wait."

"Suit yourself," dismissed shirt-guy, disappearing back into the embassy crowds only after I had signed the chit.

The lines snaking out various doors in the great entrance hall shrank over the next hour. I began to think that maybe shirt-guy was right. I had changed seats a few times just to keep the circulation going, and to change my view. There were only so many times one could read "Making a New Start in Canada" pamphlets. Or "Protecting Yourself from Disease While Abroad." Actually, I kept that one.

Twice I brightened at the appearance of a tall man at the entrance, but both times it turned out to be someone else.

The last of the snake tails disappeared through their respective doors.

A janitor appeared. The sound of his mop slopping the wet floor echoed through the hall. The tapping of single footsteps travelling from place to place stood out now with the absence of general commotion. I waited, but I was starting to feel like I was wasting my time.

An official approached with one eye on his watch to ask me if I was being looked after. He warned me they were closing their doors in ten minutes. I might as well wait the ten minutes. The janitor gave me a wary glance as he mopped around my feet. No one else was in his way.

I heard the rattle of a security guard's keys. It was time to go. I looked in the envelope for the fifth time that afternoon, at the handful of Senegalese money, the official letter, and the senior aide's business card. I let out a big sigh and headed through the glass front door that the security guard held open for me. I could be dead by morning.

"Wait!" came a cry, but it was muffled by the door shutting behind me.

The heat enveloped me like a hot pancake shawl. I stopped to catch my breath. My air-conditioned goose bumps were sweating. I'd never felt anything like it.

The door lock fiddled open behind me.

"Wait—there's a car coming for you," panted shirt-guy, leaning out on the big door but keeping both feet inside the cool building. He seemed disappointed.

"Sorry?" I had no idea what he could be talking about.

"The Swiss embassy is sending a car for you," he repeated, not quite believing it himself. "Please, come and wait inside."

124

I complied, but I wanted to hear more details.

"It seems you have important friends at their embassy," he explained, somewhat annoyed. "Someone has arranged accommodation for you at the Swiss compound until your passport and plane ticket are ready." He held his hand out.

I thought he meant to shake mine in congratulations, but he just wanted his cash back.

"They'll feed you there," he responded to my mute objection about the money.

The car came about twenty minutes later, during which I was subjected to frequent stares of curiosity from distant doorways. The Swiss vehicle was black and shiny with darkened windows. An armed driver got out and came up the steps to retrieve me. Finally, I felt safe. I couldn't wait to see Xavier—I was thrilled he'd postponed his flight until I was able to catch mine.

He wasn't waiting for me in the car, though. I asked the driver if he was waiting for me at the embassy but the driver didn't understand. I put the confusion down to the language barrier.

A woman at the embassy greeted me warmly, but made no introduction. She handed me a temporary pass to wear, and asked me to follow her inside.

The woman escorted me down several long hallways, my slapping flip-flops a sad accompaniment to the sound of her clicking heels. I felt too easily intimidated by her style—she was dressed very professionally in a light suit, and showed no signs of being bothered by the extreme heat. Her hair was dark and gathered easily on her head. She wore just a light touch of perfect make-up. She hid her examination of me well, but not completely. It was impossible to expect anyone not to wonder what situation I was emerging from. The clothes I wore had remained unchanged for almost three days. The only thing I carried was a bundle of cloth wrapped around a few pieces of aloe.

Our clicking and slapping duet echoed off the embassy corridors' neatly wood-trimmed walls. Tasteful prints of Swiss pastorals peppered the wider expanses. We passed through a breezeway—more like a clothes dryer on reverse ("It's nice when it's raining," she explained.)—and up a wide staircase where she showed me to a modest apartment. Someone had thoughtfully bought a selection of toiletries, plus a change of clothes, and left them out on the coffee table. There was a note with them.

'Salut – I hope that Alicia will buy you some nice things with the little money I have to give her. I trust that she will make you comfortable. – X'

"Are you Alicia?" I asked.

"Si." She nodded.

"Thank you."

She smiled.

"Where is Xavier?" I asked.

"He has gone to Paris," she said with the attitude of someone sharing extraneous information, like Xavier's whereabouts didn't really pertain to me.

She closed the door and left, leaving a cold emptiness behind her.

No contact numbers. No last name. He had gone home to Paris and I would never see him again.

The embassy guest apartment was a modest studio suite, the bedroom an open nook off the main space. The walls were off-white and there was nothing on them—a blank slate for temporary residents. The furniture was mostly teak and slender in proportion. A couch with two chairs and the low coffee table constituted the 'living room.' A short kitchen counter stood behind the couch, at which sat a few stools. I took a look inside the fridge. Someone, I was guessing Alicia, had brought me some fruit, cheese, and a little bread. There was also some Falken lager. I could use a beer.

But first I had to take care of how filthy I felt. A tiny bathroom was tucked between the small kitchen and the bedroom nook. Its spotless white-on-white décor left me feeling a little guilty for dragging in the dirt I carried. The rinse water ran a pungent brown until I'd washed myself at least three times. In the end I felt cleaner than after any shower I'd ever taken.

There was nothing to do once I'd explored the single room and drank my beer. There was no television. There were no books (although I read Xavier's note over and over). There was no telephone and no one to call except maybe my parents. I was happy to put that off. I decided to try on the clothes.

Alicia had bought a simple dress, a wrap skirt, and two t-shirts—all in off-white tones of cotton, all a little too loose. In the new dress, I spent a moment bouncing in the super-fluffy duvet on the bed. I played with the controls of the ceiling fan while lying back on the comfortable mattress. Before long I passed out from exhaustion, or boredom, or both.

I explored the Swiss embassy compound the next day—at least the parts I had permission to explore. I had been good about remembering to wear my pass, but the pass also stated that I was a limited guest. Busy people scattered the compound, deep in conversation or travelling from one distant corner to the next. I kept thinking I saw Xavier, but I knew my mind was playing tricks on me. I wondered why he hadn't tried to call.

I managed to find a library mid-morning. My elation was short-lived on learning that all the books were in French, German or Italian. On a high note, I found some Tintin—in French—and convinced myself it would be smart to practice the language. I ignored the gnawing feeling that it might be a waste of time, at least as far as any future with Xavier was concerned. There was still no word from him, and the more time passed the less likely it seemed that I would hear from him.

I spent two full days at the Swiss embassy, most of it in the library. My role as an object of curiosity for the library regulars was thankfully short-lived. On the second day, someone even gave me a copy of the Guardian they had picked up in town. It was mostly African news, but it was all in English. Every article was a joyful distraction—from the story about a chicken theft to an in-depth article about a small town judge who had taken bribes. I consumed every word like a sponge.

I stopped cold at a miniscule item on the back of the fifth page. *"Foreign Man Found Dead on Beach."* Was this why I hadn't heard from Xavier? I checked the date of the paper—no, we were still back in Koalack when the article was written. My terror returned when I read the details. Authorities had pieced together a theory about the partially eaten remains: the man, of South-

Asian—probably Indonesian—origin, had fallen overboard from a passing freighter. His body had washed up from the sea along the southern coastline, likely after being in the water for a day or more. My stomach curled. Was this the man who had helped us escape? Was this the body the villagers had heard rumoured? If this *was* the Indonesian, he had been murdered for aiding our escape and drifted to the coast close to where we'd landed in the life boat. Was that even possible? Yes, if the freighter had changed course to track us. If so, they really could have been on our trail once we'd landed. I crept back to my room in a trance. I took the paper with me but could not read any more. I really needed someone to talk to. A specific someone. I found a pen and paper in one of the kitchen drawers, and started writing a long letter instead.

Alicia knocked at my door at the very end of the day, just as I was forcing myself to eat a mango despite my lack of appetite. She was carrying a cell phone. There was a call coming in for me. My heart jumped—finally he was calling!

But it wasn't Xavier.

It was shirt-guy from the Canadian embassy. They had managed to push the paperwork through faster when they had learned that the next flight to Mindelo was leaving early the following morning. If I didn't catch it I would have to wait a full week for the next one, and that wasn't in anyone's budget.

So that was it then. My romantic adventure was over. Part of me couldn't wait to get out of here. I felt trapped by indifference and solitude. I wouldn't feel as safe anywhere else, but I was on my own now and the best thing to do was to keep moving. I was sure that once I left the embassy, I would be off the radar of the smugglers who allegedly hunted us. I allowed for the possibility that the continued danger was only imagined. There had been no indication that we were ever followed. If the Indonesian sailor had been murdered, it had been at sea, not on African soil. Besides, it was Xavier they were after, not me, and he was thousands of miles away in Paris. I would be well hidden on another boat in another country by the next day.

It took two minutes to pack, which left me way too much time to think. The knowledge that to leave here was to leave

128

Xavier eroded my excitement about escaping the extreme boredom. I had no permanent contact information to pass on to him—and who would do that for me? Once I was gone there would be no way for him to find me. I reminded myself with every yearning compression of my heart that he had left no contact number for me nor made any attempt to reach me while I was here. He must have known that I would feel stranded and scared. He was the one who had felt we were most in danger, and yet… The more I thought, the angrier I felt. I did not need him. I gathered the pages I had been writing to him, full of love and longing, and threw them in the trash.

My early wake-up call broke my uneasy sleep under the too-warm duvet. The black sky was just turning a hint of purple, the birds not even singing yet. I had slept already dressed, to maximize my sleep time, but the strategy had resulted in a few too many wrinkles. I quickly changed into Amadou's robe which I had since washed and hung to dry.

Alicia was at the door waiting for me, looking smart in an Italian knit dress designed with a handful of strategic gaps to conquer men and intimidate other women. I was, despite my intimidation, impressed that she had risen so early. I thanked her for all her help but she shrugged it off. She had that look again— the look of veiled curiosity. It implied more than a mild interest in the stranded Canadian woman. There was an undertone to it that hinted at something personal. It finally hit me—her relationship with Xavier was not platonic.

"You and Xavier?" I asked as she handed me a package containing my new temporary passport and my plane ticket to Mindelo.

"We are friends," she assured me, but the one-shoulder shrug that accompanied her statement implied they had been more than just friends at one time. I bet she knew his last name.

The embassy car held me like a cocoon. The tinted windows did not allow for much of a view of the streets and the driver had shut the glass between himself and the back seat. I put the handbag containing my few belongings on the seat beside me and used it as a pillow. I fell asleep immediately. I arrived at the airport having spent nearly three days in Dakar and seen nothing of it. I regretted I had missed experiencing the city but I didn't regret that Dakar had seen nothing of me. If Dakar hadn't seen me then the smugglers hadn't seen me, and maybe I would get out of here alive.

I was nervous at the check-in, but all the paperwork seemed to be in order—at least no one ushered me through a non-descript door. Maybe that was what waited for me when I landed. Sitting in the departure gate lounge I felt blatantly exposed. I had no watchful eye looking out for me—neither my Xavier's nor the Swiss or even the Canadian Embassy's. My decision to wear my Senegalese robe had backfired, giving me the sore-thumb appearance of a tourist trying to go native. I stood out like a maraschino cherry on a marble rye. I would have looked more natural in my ill-fitting European clothes. It didn't seem to matter. I was surrounded by families for the most part, and a few businessmen who were absorbed in their morning newspapers. I scoured the back of each newspaper for signs of small spy-holes, but there were none.

I knew the flight would be short, as the Cape Verde islands were only a few hundred miles away. I hoped there would be some sort of breakfast as I hadn't had anything to eat yet. The flight was in two legs—a two hour flight to Praia, followed by a short connecting flight into Mindelo where the boat was anchored. There wasn't much time between the two flights—maybe twenty minutes. Missing my connection would leave me extremely vulnerable.

The boarding call came. The families clamouring to get on first reminded me of some of the groups that had ridden with us on public transport to Dakar. The only thing missing was live chickens. My ticket placed me somewhere midway along the length of the plane, but at a window. I found my seat easily, after squeezing past a family of seven. I dropped into it, thankful for the moment of peace. As an added bonus, the seat beside mine remained empty.

I fingered the inflight magazines in the seat pocket, sorry to find none of them were in English. It would be a long flight if I had too much time to imagine all the things that could go wrong at the other end. I decided to read them as picture books.

I finished flipping through all the magazine photos and we hadn't even taken off yet. The aisles were still crowded with passengers. Everyone seemed to have one too many pieces of luggage. I found it amusing that the airline didn't take more precautions regarding baggage allowance. Up at the front of the plane—

My heart stopped.

There was Xavier. Finally.

Or was it?

My mind was playing tricks on me again. I hated these glimmers of hope that never failed to disappoint. I thought I had come to terms with never seeing him again. The familiarity seemed too tangible this time. I had to know for sure.

A grey Louis Vuitton rip-off interfered with my sight line. I craned my neck around to get a better view, but the man I'd glimpsed had already taken his seat at the front. I guessed I could have been wrong about the stature. I'd only seen Xavier wearing shorts with no shirt or, for a few brief days, a robe. This man wore a white suit. He had close shaved hair unlike Xavier's unruly waves. I'd caught a brief glimpse of part of his face but it was clean-shaven. I'd only known a man with a good amount of stubble, bordering on an actual beard. He did wear sunglasses. I strained to see the back of the man's head, willing him to turn just a little bit in my direction so I could see if he had a cut on his cheek. Then I would know…

Another man spoke instead, and the sound of his voice sent a cold shock through my veins.

"It is nice you held seat for me," announced the despised source of the voice right above my ear. I didn't need to look to know it was the Scar, but my head turned of its own accord. He was smiling his smarmiest grin. His scar was even uglier in the flat fluorescent cabin light. One hand hid in his pocket, moving inside the way I'd seen him play with his pocketed knife on the ship. Had he slipped a knife through security? I was transfixed for a moment, watching the hand lazily roll the hidden object in a slow rhythm. A faint voice in the back of my head desperately barked at me not to let him sit there. But he was already sitting down, and I was still watching his hand moving in his pocket.

"Excusez-moi…"

A late passenger had arrived, studying his ticket and the seat numbers posted above us. His actions implied that he was the legitimate assignee of what should have been the empty seat beside me. His expression was open, honestly expecting the man with the gruesome scar to forfeit his seat, or offer a reasonable explanation for being in it. He received no response.

"Excuse me," he made a second attempt, this time in careful English. "But I think that is my seat."

"My seat is back there," The Scar replied, not even looking at the man. He gestured half-heartedly towards the rear of the plane. "You can have."

"I would like you to sit here," I managed, desperately finding my voice to plead my case with this potential saviour. "I don't know this man and he is making me very uncomfortable."

"She is joking," laughed the Scar, his nervousness disguised to those who hadn't heard it before. "We are old friends."

He patted me on the leg in a gesture of camaraderie, but it had the opposite effect to the one he was hoping for.

"Don't touch me!" I shouted with a force that surprised even me. He pulled his hand off my leg like I'd burnt it, a flash of surprise crossing his face. His surprise retreated quickly behind his usual smarmy face. A flight attendant arrived within moments, on guard and ready to deal with trouble. I felt a glimmer of hope that this might even lead to his being taken off the plane. All I had to do was somehow bring attention to the knife in his pocket and he would be gone.

The Scar must have had the same thought because he had slipped out of the seat before the attendant finished her "what seems to be the problem" segue. He escaped past the attendant and disappeared into the rear of the plane out of my sight. The late passenger clarified that the Scar had been in the wrong seat, but both he and the flight attendant were eager to get settled and going.

No further investigation of the suspicious passenger seemed warranted. The attendant took my new seatmate's briefcase and shoved it into the baggage compartment above while he put on his seatbelt.

I breathed a deep sigh of relief, coaxing a warm smile from my new neighbour. I thought that I might be lucky enough after all to have some distracting conversation during the flight but the man was asleep before we had cleared the runway. I was left to bathe in the misery of my accelerating fear about what would happen when we arrived at the other end of the flight. My heart was pounding and now I had to go to the bathroom as well. The toilet would have to wait until we landed.

Chapter 13

The view below showed a great sea which glinted and sparkled in the early morning sunlight. I would normally challenge myself to spot whales in the open water, but this day found me looking for freighters. It was a fruitless game, only designed to fan the flames of my fears. Eavesdropping on conversations was another game when desperate for amusement, but the constant hum of the air circulation and the giant engines drowned out any meaning in the bits and pieces that floated over the seats. The language difference complicated the problem. There were a few English speaking passengers but not many.

I couldn't see the white-suited man at the front of the plane from where I sat, not without lifting myself high enough to be seen by unwanted eyes behind me. Now that the creepy charlatan had made his appearance and gotten away I was convinced that I had been mistaken about the tall man's identity. Xavier would never have let the Scar get so close.

My neighbour awoke with a start when we landed. He was a fairly big man, but his well-fitted business suit and kind face made him unthreatening. Big he was, however, and just the sort of obstacle I needed. I tugged at his sleeve.

"Would you mind letting me out first?" I pleaded. "I really don't want that man to follow me."

He was extremely ingratiating and not only complied but spent a good amount of time removing his briefcase from the luggage compartment so as to tie up all the passengers behind us in the cabin. He gave me a protective nod as I took a last glance back before exiting. The man in the white suit had long since departed.

I'd flown with only my tiny handbag-sized carry-on, and therefore had no need to go through the baggage claim. That would help expedite my escape from the Scar, granted everything went smoothly through customs and immigration. The airport was not a big one, but it did handle several international carriers from Europe and North America. Ours was not the only recent flight. New arrivals, even at this time of day, flooded the customs line-up. The bathroom would have to wait. Once I was through customs, I would hopefully have enough time to find the departure gate for the small plane to Mindelo. Or to find a place to hide.

I kept sneaking peaks behind me, looking for any signs of the Scar. I worried that the constant shoulder checks made me appear suspicious. Maybe raising suspicion would be a good thing, but until all my new papers proved sufficient, I did not want to encourage further international dispute.

I was pretty sure the Canadian embassy wouldn't be sending me on my way without concrete paperwork, but one always hears stories. My heart was beating in my throat, between fear of what might happen if I didn't pass through customs, and terror of what might happen if I did.

It was my turn. I took a deep breath and stepped forward, armed with a charming smile.

The customs officer asked the usual questions of how I was today and how long I was staying—the usual hard interrogation reserved for tourists. I don't know what I was worried about. I wanted to say, "Well, actually, I'm being chased by a human trafficker who wants to force me into prostitution. He's somewhere behind me in line, so if you could just…"

The stamping of my extensive paperwork by the agent echoed in my head. There were additional papers other than my temporary passport, regarding the boat and so on, but all my papers were stamped or crested with diplomatic emblems. The agent handed back my stack of approved paperwork with a blank look. He was on to the next traveller.

I tackled the next hurdle: finding my departure gate with ten minutes to spare. I checked my ticket for a gate number but saw none listed. I looked around me and discovered why. The airport was so small that I could see the departure sign for all Mindelo flights from where I stood. I stole a glance behind me and was relieved to see no sign of the Scar. I was free to go.

And free to find a bathroom! After the release of at least one pressure, this one was begging for attention. I glimpsed a washroom sign halfway down the wide hallway between myself and the area of the departure gates. With the Scar nowhere in sight, I felt safe to duck in. I could go quickly, and I felt confident that with all the other flights that had arrived I would not be in the washroom on my own.

I targeted my path towards the connecting flight gate to coincide with the pace of a large group of women heading in the same direction. I intended to use them as a decoy and slip into the bathroom as they passed the door. My brilliant plan was foiled when they all stepped into the bathroom at the same time.

On the one hand, I felt confident the Scar would not come in after me when I was surrounded by so many others. On the other hand, most of the women were ahead of me in line, and with the rest jumping the queue to join their sisters and cousins, I ended up trailing at the end. The line dragged forward at a slow crawl. I was ready to give it up when a stall finally came free. I sighed at the release.

The sense of normalcy in the activity and giggles of the group of women soothed me. I found excuses to linger at the mirror—I fixed my hair, I examined my tired eyes. I started to believe that this was like any other moment in any other bathroom. I was clinging to the calm before the storm, but I didn't want to miss my flight because of it. I followed the last of the women out.

And there standing between me and my departure gate was the ugly man who wanted me dead.

I thought I might be able to ask someone for help but the faces around me were oblivious, intent on connections and loved ones and important appointments. There wasn't enough of a crowd to hide in. There was too much of a crowd to make a run for it. I heard the word "Mindelo" trickle out of distant loudspeakers. My window of safety was narrowing fast.

The Scar had his hand in his pants pocket. His usual

mannerism of rolling his knife appeared less threatening without the billowing accompaniment of his long jacket. His current pants offered little room for movement, making it hard to imagine him attacking with ease. I tried to muster courage by imagining him as a nervous pre-schooler twiddling himself, but that just gave me the willies. There was really no getting around the knife thing.

I could see the victorious glint in his dark black eyes, hovering above his vicious grin. He stood in an attack stance, ready to cut me off if I tried to skirt around him or flee in the other direction back to the baggage claim area. I took a tentative step sideways. He mirrored it. My survival depended on maintaining the distance between us. He would easily close the gap with only 5 or 6 steps if I took my eyes off of him to search for an escape route, so we froze in a stand-off, broken only when one of us was jostled by a rushing traveller.

Shit, shit, shit.

One of us was going to have to break the impasse, and I had no brilliant plans. Nor did I want to leave the next move up to him. I could swear he stood a step closer since the last person bumped into me. How did he do that? Was that how this was going to end? Death due to obliviousness of a crowd?

I caught his step the next time I was jostled. An imperceptible shift in weight moved him a few inches towards me. He behaved like a hunter knowing not to trigger a flight response. Not that I had anywhere to fly to. But if he could shift forward, I could surely move backwards with similar guile.

I was granted an opportunity to retreat and instead backed up into a firm human-shaped wall. I gulped. I hadn't considered accomplices. But the Scar's victorious face fell flat.

"Come with me," invited that beautiful voice I thought I'd never hear again.

I looked up at the source of Xavier's voice to find myself staring at the clean-shaven face of the man I'd seen at the front of the plane. His eyes were hidden behind a smart pair of sunglasses, but from my angle I could tell that he wasn't returning my glance—his gaze was fixed on the Scar. I was confused by the mix of emotions I felt. I knew he would protect me, but why couldn't he have been here with me all along?

He didn't give me any time to react to his presence. He took my elbow in his new Velcro cast and steered me instead through the crowds heading towards the baggage claim.

"Xavier, my plane's about to leave," I protested as we headed away from where I needed to be.

"There is another flight today, later," he explained. "I will make sure you are on it."

A hint of tenderness blanketed the tension in his voice. I was more sensitive however to the fact he left himself off the departure manifesto.

Xavier put himself between me and our immediate threat. I could see The Scar following at a distance. He had been caught off guard by the sudden appearance of Xavier, and had fallen behind us a little. Xavier rarely took his eyes off of him, leaving it up to me to avoid any collision with the travellers in our way.

I threaded our way through various knots of family and friends and plaid plastic suitcases. I wasn't sure where we were meant to be going. Xavier seemed to be aiming us toward the exit, but that didn't make any sense—at least inside the airport there were security guards and police. I recalled Xavier's dislike for them. Isn't that what got us into this mess in the first place? I stopped.

"Don't stop," he warned. "It's not safe."

"It's never safe," I argued, standing my ground. He tugged at me.

"It will be," he promised.

I looked back. The Scar was gaining ground, and wore a look of determination that scattered my resolve to argue the point. We weren't far from the exit. Whatever Xavier had in mind I was willing to try it. Standing here was going to get us killed. I let him take us out the door. If it wasn't for his limping we'd have probably broken into a run.

The heat blasted us as we left the comfort of the air conditioned terminal. We were both dressed for the hot weather but the weight of it was still a shock. Now for some reason Xavier chose to stop.

"Why…?" I started, but he motioned for me to be patient as he looked around for something in the departure traffic. He grasped my hand with his good one when he spotted what he was searching for, and pulled me along the sidewalk to a cab several hundred feet beyond the head of the line. He signalled to someone behind us while he held the cab door open for me. I paused before climbing in to see what he was gesturing at.

"Vite! Vite!" He urged.

I shot him a nasty look. He may have had a plan but I didn't like being shuffled around, and I disliked being barked at even more. I felt bad after seeing the hurt expression on his face, but I did not move as quickly as he hoped.

"Please," he added, and climbed in after me whether I moved fast enough or not. I scooted over underneath his scrambling limbs. The cab pulled away from the curb even before the car door shut.

I scoured the crowds behind us through the rear window of the cab. I spotted the Scar easily, climbing into a similar cab in the distance. He pointed directly at us as he spoke to the driver. We had not escaped fast enough. Maybe our driver could lose him.

Xavier directed the driver using a patois I had never heard before. The language was not English or French or particularly African-sounding. He conversed for a good length with the driver in serious tones. I couldn't follow any of the conversation except that they both seemed to be familiar with Xavier's intentions. The driver reassured Xavier about something while keeping close watch on the other taxi in his rear-view mirror. I guessed that the driver knew we were trying to shake the guy. I hoped our driver was clever enough to lose the other cab.

"Are you ok?"

I was so focused on the driver and the car behind us that at first I didn't realize Xavier was talking to me. He took my hand and that got my attention.

"No, not really," I said, and pulled my hand away. A flicker of disappointment crossed his face but with his eyes hidden behind sunglasses I could have been mistaken about that. I was sorry I had removed myself from his attempt to reach out but it was too late to put my hand back. His gaze was fixed on mine. I looked away and found myself returning the rear-view glance of the cab driver. He examined me with curiosity. I wished he'd put his focus back on the car we were trying to ditch.

"Are you sorry I am here?" he asked with the tone of someone who was afraid of getting the wrong response. He took my hand a second time, as if it had fallen away by accident.

"No," I returned his hidden gaze. "No, I'm not. I just... thought it was over."

I meant more than just the threat.

I stole a side-glance at the driver through the mirror. His focus was back on the road.

"It was good I returned to Paris," said Xavier, ignoring my subtle invitation to talk about where we stood. "I had to make arrangements, and I could not make them from Dakar."

I saw Xavier and the driver exchange glances. He was obviously not telling me everything. I didn't know if he was hiding the truth from me or from the cab driver.

"And I have a good doctor in Paris," Xavier continued, as if those were the arrangements he was referring to. "Do you not think that I look much better?"

I did, but there was too much unknown for me to submit to his dry humour. I grunted and turned around in my seat to keep an eye on the car that followed. He let go of my hand and rubbed his face with those long slender fingers.

The car wound away from the airport traffic, the tour vans, and the airport hotels. We turned onto a road which rose gradually above the congestion of the small capitol into a sparse arid landscape. The brightly painted colonial buildings thinned out as we climbed away from the main road. The open space near the top of the hill made us visible from a great distance. There were no other cars driving up here—just the faint cloud of dust which followed us at a distance. Our own cloud of dust made it impossible to lose our shadow. I wondered how Xavier was planning on escaping from the Scar's chasing cab. Maybe there was jungle over the crest of the hill?

The landscape opened up even further when we reached the

top. Mountains peaked in the distance and the island's soft volcanic soil between them had eroded into fantastic chasms. Patchy agriculture plastered the spaces below. I looked behind us to see the ocean stretching away. The late-morning sun glinted on the tiny waves in the distance.

A private drive met our road at a T-junction past the crest of the hill. A small hut and a few worn trucks were visible further away down the private drive, but there were no people anywhere. Just beyond the intersection a small stand of shrubs and thick palm trees stood guard. The trees were alone in the landscape and formed an unusual clump on either side of the road. Our taxi drove past the stand of trees before slowing to a crawl. Xavier reached for my hand again, gripping it tight this time. Whatever the plan was, it was going down now. I observed him for clues. His eyes were fixed on the taxi that followed.

The dust from the other taxi billowed across the top of the hill behind us. The taxi slowed when it was within sight of us, coming to a crawl that matched our pace. It stopped near the intersection with the private drive, maintaining the gap between us.

Xavier said something in the patois to the driver, and we sped forward a little. The Scar's taxi jumped forward to follow, and slid into the shadows under the cluster of palms. We stopped. The other cab stopped.

I looked at Xavier, then at the face of the driver in the mirror. Their eyes were both glued to the car behind us. There was no sign from either of them that we would be moving ahead any time soon. Xavier's fingers, where his cast would allow, tapped lightly against his white pant leg. Anxiety permeated the interior of the cab, and still, we waited, transfixed. The taxi behind us held its position in the shade of the trees, its motor idling, waiting for our next move.

The trees moved first.

Several armed men emerged from the foliage and surrounded the Scar's taxi—two in front, two behind, and the rest on either side. They aimed their rifles at the passenger in the back seat. The driver was shouting in panic—even from our distance we could hear his pleading.

One of the two men in front indicated the driver should exit the cab. The frightened man opened the car door, but one of the other men at the driver's side quickly kicked it shut with his foot. The two armed men shouted at each other but resolved their differences right away. The second gunman stepped back to let the driver out once more, this time demanding that the driver turn the engine off and hand over the keys. The Scar tried to grab at the driver but had missed his chance. Four of the gunmen stepped up to the cab and opened the remaining doors, shouting and motioning at the Scar to get out. He wouldn't.

"Do they know he carries a knife?" I whispered.

"I don't think that's going to…"

Xavier's response was cut short by the sharp crack of gunfire. The sound echoed against our shortened breathes. The man who had fired into the car reached in and dragged a struggling figure out. The Scar was still alive but there was blood all over his hand and sprayed across his shirt.

"Bon. C'est la même main," I heard Xavier growl beside me. It was unusual to hear such contempt in his voice. My stomach turned at the glimpse into what The Scar must have done to him while he had Xavier imprisoned in the hull of the freighter. I felt guilty at not fully appreciating Xavier's stakes in the fate of the monster behind us, stakes that went beyond avenging the death of his brother.

Chapter 14

The pathetic cries of the injured Scarab were muffled by the closed windows and circulating air of our taxi. I fought any pangs of pity for him as the armed men dragged him away from the shade of the trees and down the road to the distant cluster of trucks. One of the men stayed with the cab driver, but his rifle was now slung over his back and he was counting out money into the driver's quivering upturned palm.

"Senhor?"

The driver's voice tore our attention away from the drama outside and back to what should happen now that we were free. Yes—what now?

Xavier asked the driver to wait a moment. He still gripped my hand with his good one and my fingers seemed to become very interesting to him. I couldn't help him out because I was at a complete loss about where he was coming from at this moment. I didn't know where we could go from here, apart from simply returning to the airport and going our separate ways. I wished things were different, but after the prolonged silence at the embassy I was afraid to expect anything more.

"You have need to take your plane soon," he began. At least I hoped it was a beginning. "I would like to come with you…"

I held my breath for the qualification I sensed would follow.

"… but I am not welcome to stay in Cabo Verde. I must take a flight back to Paris."

So this was it, then. My heart sank into the emptiness left

by his statement.

Xavier's glance flicked to the driver's watching eyes in the rear-view mirror and back. His glance communicated more than wariness at the driver's eavesdropping on our lovers'—former lovers, I corrected—conversation. It seemed Xavier did not feel at complete liberty to say what he wanted.

"I hope that…," he continued with faintly disguised difficulty. "I would like to spend time with you before you leave. I have a house here—it was a gift for my brother. A wedding gift. It is not finished, but it is private. We can go there, until it is time for your plane. If you like."

It was his turn to hold his breath. I had every reason to go straight to the airport. Not only had I just watched a man be paraded to his probable death but I had been kept in the dark about my involvement in the plan to make it happen. This man whom I thought I loved, who had used me as bait, showed no indication that he wanted more than a quick farewell. I still had no contact number, had been asked for none—I did not even have a full name. Once I was on the plane to Mindelo, I could leave the entire adventure behind and go back to my real life of crying in a heap on the floor. At least there I'd be responsible for my own misery. Or so my mind argued.

My body and heart took a different position. The lust that had been dampened by fear now gushed like hot lava through my veins. To be alone with him would be to… I wanted him to tear off my clothes right there in the cab. I lifted his sunglasses and discovered a pair of desperate eyes fixed on mine. Maybe I was wrong about how he felt. Maybe it didn't matter if it was only one last time.

"Let's go to your house," I blurted, squeezing his hand.

His face softened immediately, reflecting a warm glow of relief. His gorgeous smile returned.

Xavier gave directions to the driver, who made a well-crafted U-turn in the dry dirt road. We drove back through the stand of trees and past the private drive. There was no sign that anything unusual had occurred there just five minutes before. The worn trucks that had stood by the out-building were gone. Not

144

even a cloud of dust remained.

"There's one thing," I insisted, in lieu of all I'd been through.

"Oui?" Xavier had been lost in thought down the distant driveway, but turned back to me.

"I want your phone number."

"But I gave all my numbers to you, everything." He seemed honestly confused.

"No, you didn't," I insisted, shaking my head. I would know.

"Yes, I left everything with…"

He started to laugh openly, shaking his head at some private joke.

"…Alicia," he finished.

"I knew it!" I declared. That bitch.

"But she was nice to you, yes?" He was concerned he had misjudged his "friend" in other regards.

"Yes, she was nice," I conceded. "Polite. She did bring me some clothes, despite what I'm wearing. Nice ones. And other stuff, too." I indicated my little carry-on bag on the floor.

"A toothbrush?"

"Yes," I giggled.

"Good," he sighed, leaning back in the seat and staring out the taxi window in the other direction. "When you did not call me, I thought that you had finished with me. I would not be surprised. I have put you in terrible danger." He shot me a look of heavy guilt. He was right—the string of life-threatening experiences should have been more than enough to put me off him. I was so relieved, though, that he had been fighting the same doubts I had struggled with alone in Dakar that I was willing to forgive a lot.

"When you didn't call," I admitted, "I thought you'd had it with me. I was sure you were congratulating yourself on being safe in Paris, partying it up with much sexier women—pretty much forgetting about me altogether."

"Forgetting? No!"

"But sexier women…"

"No, no sexier women."

He acted a little offended, but relaxed when it sank in that I was teasing him. Mostly.

"You are the sexiest woman," he added, flashing a coy smile from his relaxed position next to me. He lifted my hand to his lips and kissed it with the utmost tenderness. A burst of warmth spread through me, setting my skin on fire. He let go and rested his hand on my leg like that was its natural spot. The light touch of his fingers caressing my leg through the light fabric of my dress sent shivers straight up between my legs.

I nestled against him and his fine white linen suit. He told me about his short visit home. He had gone straight to the hospital from the airport, and spent most of the first day there getting x-rayed and then patched up. The police had come by to take a report for his insurance. They had given him the same attitude about the strange Canadian woman he had picked up as the Canadian embassy had given me about him. The similarity made us both laugh. He had also spoken to a trusted colleague—a rarity—at Interpol, as promised, about the true nature of our experience.

The taxi's route around the many tight corners of the hills above Praia pressed us together in the backseat and coaxed smiles from us. Our path wound down the hill part way and then back up above the harbour where a residential neighbourhood curved around the shore opposite the busy town waterfront. We entered a barren street lined with empty concrete buildings. The taxi stopped.

The driver turned in his seat to have a short conversation with Xavier, who then handed him a wad of bills. The driver took the money and nodded. He let the engine idle while we exited the cab. I climbed out after Xavier and the taxi slipped away the moment I shut the car door behind me.

There were few sounds around us except for an ocean breeze whispering through the tin roofing of the abandoned buildings. There was nothing and no one up here.

"Where are we?" I asked.

I wasn't taking a step further without more explanation.

"Vas-y," coaxed Xavier, wrapping his good arm around my stubborn shoulders. "I told you, yes, that the house was not

146

finished?"

"Yes…"

I hobbled with him around the side of a concrete block cube that at some point had been destined for life as a garage. A broken path led down some steps and across a secluded yard littered with fallen piles of pilfered building materials. Another concrete block structure framed the yard at the opposite end, large holes punching the building's walls where windows should have been. Heavy plastic sheeted the windows on the lower floor. The windows above were open to the sky—only the frame of the roof had been completed. A wide concrete plinth stretched along the width of the building's base, presumably the foundation for what would have been a deck.

Xavier hopped up onto the once-future patio, and extended a hand to help me do the same. I laughed that even with only one good leg and a broken rib he was more agile than I was.

A large piece of plywood blocked what might have been intended as a back entrance to the house. It was locked in place with a combination padlock. Xavier removed the lock and held the sheet of plywood open for me.

"Are you serious?" I asked.

"It is not as bad as you think," he answered. "The finished part is on the other side of the house."

I wasn't convinced.

The open plywood "door" revealed a long unfinished hallway. Sheets of plastic hung over further door-sized openings on either side of the hallway, sheltering more unfinished spaces. The hallway ended at what appeared to be a balcony above a room that rose from the unseen floor below. A series of holes on the far exterior wall were covered in fluttering translucent material which I assumed to be a variation on the plastic sheeting theme. The bright sunlight streaming into that part of the house made the material difficult to distinguish. Xavier promised that was the "good" part of the house, and urged me to go ahead of him.

True to Xavier's word, the balcony at the end of the hallway unveiled a different world. This was the space that the builders had finished. A white terrazzo floor covered the large area of a double-height main room. The combination of white tile floor and unpainted white plaster walls caused the room to literally glow in the light from the big windows. The translucent material I'd seen fluttering had not been plastic but white gauze curtains blowing in the ocean breeze. The windows framed a view high above the city harbour and a glittering ocean spotted with white sails and fishing boats. A set of curved stairs descended into the room from the balcony where we stood. I felt as if invited to enter a play.

The room was sparsely furnished. A small rattan couch with ivory cushions sat against the wall at the bottom of the stairs. A plate of food and a bucket of chilled wine had been set out on a matching table next to it. The only other piece of furniture in sight was a queen-sized bed placed squarely in the middle of the room like a bold statement. Expensive linens hugged the bed on all four sides, under a pair of voluptuous pillows.

I was dumbstruck. Were we in a house or in a TV brothel?

Xavier stopped behind me at the top of the stairs. He rested his hands on my hips and surveyed the room. He started giggling. So I wasn't the only one who found the setting absurd.

"Why are *you* laughing?" I prodded. "Isn't this your house?"

"I have not been here in a long time," he sighed. "I did not know what to expect."

"I don't understand," I said, melting when he kissed the back of my neck. "Is this part of the arrangements you were talking about or is the house always like this? Why is only part of the house finished?"

"When the house was being built," Xavier murmured between his hot kisses, "my brother… and his fiancée… lived… at her father's house …it was difficult. They asked for this room to be finished first… so that they… could be alone together."

"But that was…"

"That was a long time ago, yes," he agreed. He pulled away from kissing my neck and held me instead, like it gave him strength to get through his story. "It is three years, I think. I tried to sell the house but Mercado threatened anyone who tried to buy it.

He wanted to know that I would remember. But how could I forget?

"So, the house sits and rots. The furniture has been stolen—this furniture is new. Thieves have taken the doors and the windows, the hardware—most of the materials. I would not have come back here but it is the only place I know that I can be alone with you. I hoped that you would want to come here. I hoped. I asked Mercado to clean it up, for you, just in case. He has been too obvious about what we might want to be alone for, but I did not expect him to be so kind. He hates me very much."

"Who's Mercado?"

"Sophie's father," he answered. He winced when he said her name.

His hands fell away from the embrace as he slipped past me and trotted down the stairs. 'Who's Sophie?' I mouthed after him although I already knew. His flash Parisian shoes clicked on the tile steps when he bounced down them, leaving the name hanging in the air behind him. He dropped into the rattan couch and snatched the wine bottle by the neck from its silver cask.

"What kind of wine did that bastard take out of his cellar for us?" he mused.

The drips from the fast melting ice swung a wide arc across the floor in front of him. He leaned forward to avoid getting wet. A smile erupted when he examined the label.

"So he has not been generous after all," he announced, laughing. He looked up. "What are you doing over there? Come and drink some cheap wine."

I made my grand entrance into the palatial white room. The cheap Senegalese flip-flops I wore slapped on the tile floor and echoed against the flat walls. Xavier had traded his sunglasses for the opener on the side table and mid-uncorking glanced up, surprised by the noise. The sound of the cork popping distracted both of us from the flopping of my shoes. By the time I reached Xavier, he was taking a long swig of wine, eyes closed, and had forgotten all about my donated shoes.

He handed me the bottle. I drank a cold delicious mouthful of the cheap wine, its tartness a great companion to his renewed focus on my body. I fit myself between his knees at an easy distance from his promising embrace. I was happy to let his plastered hand pull me close to him by the waist. He buried his face in my middle and dropped his hands to my ass. I absently ran my fingertips along his short-cropped scalp—the short hair felt great. His hands caressing my ass felt great. He snuck his good hand under the hem of my dress and pulled at my underwear until it fell to the floor. I spilt a gulp of wine down my chin.

Xavier tugged the bottle away from my lips.

"Save some for me," he laughed and stood to drink. He pressed me tighter against him, and I could feel him getting hard. He replaced the bottle in the cask after another quenching gulp or two.

"Hey. There's still…"

He dodged my words with a fabulous kiss. I gave in. There were more urgent cravings to be sated.

He lifted me off my feet and carried me in his arms the few steps to the bed. His continuing heavy kisses muffled my delighted shriek. Deep affection transcended my amusement when he laid me down very gently and climbed onto the bed with me. I thrilled in rediscovering his body and the touch of his renewed and prolonged caresses. His deep blue-violet eyes drank in every inch of me. I couldn't wait to get naked with him.

"Aren't you hot in that jacket?" I asked, pushing a corner of it off his shoulder.

"Did you say that I am hot?" he joked, wriggling his good arm out of the sleeve.

"No," I teased, watching as he sat up to tug the other sleeve over his cast. He stopped.

"No?"

He absently shook at the sleeve while holding my gaze, waiting for my clever response. But the cast was too clumsy for the sleeve to slip off easily, and the jacket became stuck. With his eyes fixed on mine, he shook his arm harder and harder without succeeding in freeing himself. The effort was finally too much and he tore his attention away from me to yank the jacket off and toss it at the sofa. I let out a quiet snort as he recovered his composure.

"I think that you are laughing at me," he observed, turning back to me.

"I'm not, I promise." I swore, but then laughed out loud.

"We will see if it is as easy to take off your dress."

He was crawling all over me before I knew what was happening. His hands pulled and tugged my dress in all directions but off. He tickled me in spots I would never have guessed were so vulnerable. I succumbed to the joy of the merciless attack, howling underneath him. He eased up so I could catch my breath.

"Are you sure you're not laughing at me?" he asked.

"Positive," I swore, panting. I stared up at his sincere expression. My protesting hands relaxed against his muscular arms and I revelled at the silky feel of his skin.

He shifted his weight to his elbows, pressing his body against mine as he did so. The soft warmth of his lips curled my toes when he took my hand and kissed my palm. I let my fingers slip into his mouth. He suckled them before pinning my hand above my head.

"Truce?" he asked.

"Maybe," I grinned, brushing the tangled hair out of my eyes so that I could return his gaze.

His other hand swept against my thighs and crawled up under the length of my dress. The steady warmth that had been gnawing between my legs since that moment in the cab burst into a full blown heat. My legs parted in an open invitation to his fingers as he played inside the moistening folds between them. I grabbed at Xavier's shoulder with a gasp of surprise, gripping a tight handful of his t-shirt in my fist. He grinned triumphantly and met my open mouth with a hungry kiss, pushing his tongue against mine in a dance to make up for lost time.

I was so hungry, so wet, and so eager to have him inside me that I practically cried when his fingers slipped out to undo his pants. I heard the zipper slide and felt the soft linen push away, leaving the raw hard heat of him against my skin. I tucked my toes against the waistband as he struggled to get his pants off, and did my best to help. He shook his head and pushed my legs out wider, guiding himself inside me with his good hand, pressing his hips up firm against mine. I moaned as he sank inside me, filling me, satisfying that emptiness that missed him so. His warm breath quickened against my cheek and he squeezed my hand so hard it hurt.

Xavier moved in me as if he were caressing me from the inside. I arched my head back into the pillow and closed my eyes as his slow but steady thrusts triggered rising waves of euphoria. His hot kisses moved across my neck, his teeth grazing against my skin with tentative bites. I pushed hard against him as my body began to tremble underneath his. He picked up his speed.

I flung my eyes open to catch his darkened gaze. His mouth hung open slightly as he struggled to catch his quickened breath, and one corner of his sensuous lips twitched up when he caught me looking. He pulled my hand loose from where I gripped his now stretched t-shirt, and briefly engulfed my fingers in his open mouth. He guided my hand between our pressed bodies and pushed my wet fingers in a circle against my clit.

The hint of extra pressure against my ready-to-explode bud as he sped up faster still shot a hard pulse through me so intense it came out of my mouth as a scream. He laughed as I shuddered under him and dug my toes into the backs of his thighs with another surrendering cry. His laughter cut short when his own orgasm sprung with equal surprise. He fell against me, covered in sweat and beaming like a canary-fed cat.

Our fingers idled together above our heads while we caught our breath, laughing.

I marvelled at how well Xavier had recovered since I'd last seen him. The hospital had replaced Amadou's gruesome stitches with invisible ones. The gash they held together was healing nicely but would definitely leave a scar. The worst of the bruising had faded dramatically—I wouldn't have even noticed it if I hadn't known the bruises were there. I mulled over the crisp new look that he'd returned to me with. Xavier's clean shave and short, short haircut were just as striking as his laid-back look had been, maybe more so. He met my perusal with a questioning look.

"I love the way you fuck me," I said in response.

"I can tell," he teased.

152

I swung at him in mock reproach.

"Attention," he giggled, catching my hand with little effort. "I am an injured man."

His sweet giggle faded as his focus shifted to the hand he now held. He sighed, his thoughts drifting off a time and place long before I existed for him. It must have been difficult to return to a place with such bittersweet memories. How much time had he spent here with his brother and future sister-in-law before they were killed? Was it here that he'd slept with her? I wondered that he could come back to the house at all.

"I'm sorry we have to be together in a place that has such sad memories for you," I said.

"There are good memories, also," he assured me.

"Do you think they would have approved? I mean, of us being here?"

"They would approve, yes. Very much."

He smiled to himself from somewhere far away.

"I'm sorry I didn't get to meet them," I continued.

"I am sorry, as well. Bastian—my brother... you would have liked him. He was very funny, and gentle. Everybody liked him. And he would have been happy to know you.

"Sophie, euh, I do not know. She did not like to share the attention. She was always needing to be at the centre. She was accustomed to having everyone's eyes to be on her—men, at least, could not look away. She was very beautiful and she knew how to make her beauty work for her. But perhaps you would have liked her anyways. She had much energy and life."

The way he spoke of her prompted the question that had weighed on me for days—the one that had tormented me all those long dark hours in the floating steel trap—to come spilling out uninvited.

"Wasn't it hard for you?" I asked. Oh, God. I couldn't come right out and say it. His affair wasn't any of my business. Maybe I could change the subject before he knew what I meant. But I was consumed by the need to know if he still loved her—if his love for her stood in the way. At least I still had a chance to soften the question before I ruined everything. "I mean, being in love with the same woman as your brother?"

He sat up, surprised, staring at me like I'd stung him.

"What do you mean? How do you think that I was in love with Sophie?"

"I... It's just..."

I didn't want to mention the Scar, who had obviously been filling my head with lies and topping it up with half-truths. I was ashamed I'd taken anything he'd said at face value. The intensity with which Xavier stared at me made me want to take the question back, but it was too late.

"I'm sorry," I murmured. I turned away. I couldn't stand the way he was looking at me.

"Did *he* tell you that?" He didn't need to clarify whom. "What did he tell you?"

With a tender hand he turned my face back to his. He held on until I met his gaze.

"It doesn't matter," I said, not sounding convinced. "He was just trying to fuck me up, wasn't he?"

Xavier closed his eyes. He lay back down on the bed and let all the guilt and pain seep out of his lungs.

"I will tell you," he said, finally. "I will tell you the story of my brother, and me, and Sophie Mercado. If I do not tell you the story, I think that you will always wonder. If I do not tell you, you will only know our story from the mouth of a monster."

Chapter 15

Xavier squeezed my hand and smiled with sad eyes as he launched into the tale of the mysterious woman who had caused me such anxiety, the intimidating Sophie Mercado.

"I met Sophie when I was at school. She was—how do you say... 'boarded'? Boarded, oui. My mother died after a long illness, and my brother was sent back to Switzerland. My father agreed to let me stay in my mother's apartment in Paris so that I would finish my schooling. I think that he had fears that I would run away if he had not let me stay. I studied at the same school as Sophie. We were both, uh, difficult students."

I laughed at this, and he shot me a reproaching sideways glance. Then he laughed with me.

"We were difficult, yes. We drank very much. We broke her out of school late in the night. We fooled around also. Her father learned this and he was very angry. He came to the school to pay me money. To go away."

"Really?"

"Yes," he assured me, his eyes widening at the memory. "I would not take his money. He threatened to take Sophie home to Cape Verde, but she refused, of course. Alors, he cut off her funds. No more money."

"Wow."

"Wow, yes. Pauvre Sophie. She stayed with me but she was used to money. I only had a little. And we were no good together."

"But you were together..."

"Together for the wrong reasons. We were teenaged marmots with no responsibility. We did not see ourselves as a boyfriend and girlfriend. No. We fought all the time. About money. About school. About me. I started to hate her. Almost. But we had never been in love. We just fell in together. I felt so guilty. I felt responsible for her situation. I tried to convince her to ask her father to help her, but she refused. And we fought about that.

"I had some money for school but it was not enough to pay for both of us. This is when a friend began to offer me money to help him out with some things. He was very small, shy, and very rich, and I think, he was a target of crueller classmates. He had soirées at his house and his friends—they were not his friends—they would help themselves to his things. He paid me to steal them back. I became good at the recovery. And I became good at, uh, talking."

"What do you mean, 'talking'?"

"I could talk myself out of difficulty." He shrugged, the corners of his mouth twitching up slightly. "I think, also, I was not afraid. I got a rush when I found the things that had been taken from my friend—his camera, a watch, those kinds of things. Sometimes I would get caught stealing back from the thief, but it did not matter—I would laugh and get out.

"When we finished school, I thought the fun of adventure was over. I worked at a record store; I was trying to make enough money to pay for Sophie to stay in Paris. Things were very difficult. She would not look for a job. My brother came to Paris to school also, and he was offering his school money to help. It was no good. I told her to go home, but she was always so much drama. Always drama. Then my shy friend from school called. He said, 'I have a job for you.' He wanted that I move to Algiers with him, because he had lost something else, something big, but… that is a different story.

"So, what could I do? I gave Sophie money to go home. She threw it back at me and said it was over. She said she had stayed only to make me more miserable, because she hated me that much. She said that she was going to stay with a friend, and she said that she never wanted to see me again. And she walked out before I did."

"Was the friend your brother?"

"What? No... there was no friend. She came back with her key the moment that I left for the airport. She had nowhere else to go. So my brother had a big surprise when he came to stay at our mother's apartment. He was needing a quiet place to study. But, instead, he found a crying woman."

"So she was in love with you, at that point?"

"No! She was pregnant!"

"Oh, no..."

"Yes. But she did not have the baby. I did not learn about the pregnancy—or l'avortement—until much later. It is probable that it was not mine."

"Your brother's?"

"No," he dismissed that idea. "There were other men."

I raised my eyebrows at him.

"Yes, she slept around," he confirmed. "But she always came home after she had finished with her lovers. I wished often that she did not, but... I could not ask her to leave. It is possible, maybe, that the baby was mine. We were living together so sometimes we would sleep together. It was convenient. It was like... a bad habit. So it is possible. But I don't think so."

"But your brother wouldn't keep the pregnancy a secret, would he? The way you've spoken about him..."

"He would have told me, yes. But she lied to my brother, also. She told him that I knew about it."

"Oh...."

"My brother was thinking that I must have had a good reason to go away. But my brother is... was... a very good man, and he would look after the pregnant woman. My brother... he was different with Sophie. She liked to, uh... she needed to have her way. But my brother, he would say, "No." No one ever said no to Sophie. I never said no to her. I think that is why she fell in love with him."

"Did you find them together, when you got home?"

"No. He would not sleep with her. She tried. And she was used to having who she wanted. But he would not. I told him to— we had spoken many times by telephone while I was away. I told him it was over, and that if he liked her he should sleep with her.

He told me that he was not interested. I thought that maybe he had another girlfriend. But truly he did not like her."

"So what happened?"

"He called her father."

"No!"

"Yes, he did!" Xavier broke out laughing. He looked at me, grinning. "Sophie's father is the only man I have ever had fear of, but my brother looked through her things for his telephone number, and told him to come to Paris and to get his daughter.

"And M. Mercado, he loved my brother immediately. My brother was quiet, and honest, and sincere, and intelligent. He was studying to be anthropologist. He was very steady. And Sophie, she would do what my brother told her to do—M. Mercado had never seen that. Imagine this: when my brother told Sophie to go home with her father, she did."

"But... how did they end up together, then?"

"It was five years later; I met Sophie in Barcelona, in a club. She was very drunk, and a man was following her and would not leave her alone. She would not have spoken to me, but she was in trouble with this man. I got rid of him and we stayed up the rest of the night together. I insisted that she drink coffee. She insisted that I tell about my brother. I was surprised. I had not known that she loved him. I joked to her that we had at last found something that we both agreed. And for the second time we became friends."

"You hooked up again?" I was surprised by this turn of events. But I misunderstood.

"Not lovers," Xavier corrected me. "Friends. Like when we began our school. This time we parted on good terms, and when I returned home I told my brother the story. Bastian was very interested. He was very interested in her interest."

"He'd changed his mind."

"He had changed his mind, yes. But he refused to call her. So I did what an older brother should do. I sent him on vacation for his birthday. Also, I arranged that Sophie would arrive at the same time. They did not spend a day apart after that holiday."

"So you were a good brother."

"But, he was a better brother."

158

"It couldn't have been your fault, what happened."

Xavier looked at me with great tenderness, caressed my face, but shook his head.

"It was my fault. I brought trouble to their home. I knew I was being followed by a sick, violent man but I did not want to miss the wedding of my only brother."

"I'm sure your brother would have been really hurt if you did."

"Yes, that is true—but he would be alive."

"Oh, God, Xav—I'm sorry."

"It happened immediately after the wedding. I think. I do not know for certain. They just... disappeared. No one could find them. We thought they were being a new couple, but after more than four days with no word... I came to the house—this one—and there was a single note, it was nailed to the wall inside of the door. It said, 'Next time, you will think twice.' I was sick. I knew I would not see them again. My brother's body was found later. Never Sophie, but I know that she is dead, also."

"But couldn't it have had to do with Sophie's father? I mean, those guys at the taxi—they weren't exactly having a tea party."

Xavier offered me a sad smile.

"This island belongs to Julio Mercado," he explained. "No one would dare to touch him. No. I knew who was responsible. It was confirmed to me much later. And M. Mercado also knew the very moment I told him that I had found the note. He put a gun to my head and he cocked it. He held it there but I would not look away from him. I knew he hated me already. I think that if he knew that his daughter had been pregnant while she lived with me I would be dead. But finally he dropped his gun. He turned his back and told his men to take me to the airport. He told me that if I ever came to CV again I would be dead."

"Except for just this once..."

"Just this once, to pay the debt I owed."

"And now it's paid, you still have to go?"

"Yes," he said, glancing at his watch. "But not yet."

We lay together with his story hanging over our heads. His

life. I didn't speak for a long time, out of respect for his thoughts. His hands wandered absently across me, caressing here and there from some distant place in his memories.

"So that's why you didn't want to meet up with my uncle in Mindelo," I burst, sitting up with the excitement of having solved a piece of his puzzle.

"That is why, oui," he confirmed, tugging me back down.

"Xav…," I murmured, consumed by darker thoughts. "You knew he was out there, on the ocean. You said you didn't expect to find him. Is that true? That was such a coincidence… It's hard to believe you weren't hunting him down."

"No," he whispered. "I never wanted to see him. That was very much a strange coincidence. A bad coincidence. I was trying to leave Grand Canaria so that I could avoid him. I did not want to take the chance."

"It figures," I snorted.

"What figures?" He raised an eyebrow, thinking I meant to insult him.

"Irony," I explained.

"Bfff," he retorted. "I would have preferred gold."

I agreed.

The room heated up as the morning breeze from the ocean died down. I heated up as he played with the crumpled fabric resting against my body. Trickles of sweat rolled down my skin.

"I have to take this dress off," I announced.

"Ok," he smiled, pulling his hands away to give me some space.

I instinctively turned toward him when I sat up to lift the dress up over my head. I surfaced from under the dress to find Xavier sitting up opposite me, his hands sliding up over my breasts the moment they were exposed to him. My nipples reached out to him, welcoming him like a long-lost friend. I ran my fingers down his flexing arms, squeezing them tight in response. He took my dress from me and flung it to join his jacket on the sofa. His t-shirt was the only barrier left between our naked selves.

I tugged his shirt up over his head. Xavier did his best to help by pulling his arms through but I had to get up on my knees above him to finish the job. Once his shirt was free and he found himself face-to-face with his dear pillowy friends he lost no time in acquainting them with his lips. I leaned into him as he teased each nipple with his clever tongue. The touch of his wet lips shook me alive. I savoured the sensation of his silky skin finally meshing with my own.

I kissed the top of his short-cropped head—tender kisses born from awareness of the long absence that must follow. I ran my hands across the brush of his hair and down to his rippling shoulders. His hands shifted from their place above my waist to grip my ass tightly. One hand came back but the other let a finger trace the line that ran down the small of my back, down between my legs and all the way through to my clit where it stopped to play. I moaned into him, melting forward and losing my balance.

He leaned back with me until he was lying flat on the bed. He pulled my hips forward with his momentum until his tongue could play where his fingers had been. He was smart enough to hold my hips above the place where his ribs had broken, because once his tongue was at play I was lost to the moment. I arched back, gasping. He was covering ground he wanted to remember, tasting every little piece of me, inside and out.

Behind me my hand found his cock and grasped it. He was already hard but I stroked him as his tongue stroked me, squeezed him as his hands squeezed my ass. He moaned as I moaned. I pulled myself away from his mouth and shifted my hips down to straddle him, ignoring his sigh. I leaned over him to catch his wide gaze as I guided his hard cock inside of me. I squeezed him from the inside. He pulled me to him, face buried in my neck with a start. He groaned, pushing the hair back from my face. I moved on him with the same gentleness he had shown earlier, delighting in every sensation, wanting it to last forever. We smiled together.

I ground my hips into his, pushing him in deeper, until he was in as far it was possible for him to go.

"Oh, God," he cried, in French, of course, and grabbed tightly at my thighs.

My hips swayed in and out, fucking him tenderly at first. I watched his eyes close at the sensual delight, his face distorting with each wave. I was soon breathing fast with him, trying to keep up the motion as my body ramped into overdrive. I angled my hips forward, driving harder into his pelvic bone to give my clit a better ride. He was gasping now, but so was I. I heard myself let out a high-pitched cry. I looked up to find his gaze locked to mine as I kept going, harder, chasing the cresting waves. He reached for one of my dangling breasts, found the nipple, and pinched it hard. That did it for me.

"Oh god oh god oh god," I shrieked. There was nothing else to say. I was coming and going and coming around again. I lurched forward into him, pressing my pelvic bone against his to sustain the shooting sensation that flooded through me. He came at the same time, his hips pushing up to meet mine in response. He shuddered beneath me, his tight grip loosening on my legs. I collapsed into him with satisfied exhaustion.

I snaked my arms around his neck. He held me tight to him and breathed me in deeply.

The room, too, embraced us.

"I don't want you to go," I whispered into his ear.

His chest pressed against mine with each of his breaths.

"Will you come to Paris? After your voyage?" he asked, not moving otherwise.

Visiting Paris was a given. I thought he'd never ask.

"To live?" he added.

Could I move to Paris? It would mean giving up the pathetic life I knew and embarking on a completely unknown future. It would mean relying on him entirely until I could learn to speak French properly. It would mean getting to know Paris. It would mean getting to know him. Could I even consider turning him down? No—but it was such a big commitment that I really needed to think the proposal through more fully.

"Yes," I said. It just sort of came out.

His body relaxed under my embrace. It was a huge deal, but to discuss it further would be to ruin the moment. In a couple of hours or so we would be whisked to the airport and I would be sailing away with family back to another lifetime. There was a very good chance the moment would pass into myth and life would

162

carry on as before.

"Xavier?" I mumbled into his shoulder.

"Hmmmmm?"

"I still don't have your phone number."

His body shook against mine. The hollow cage of his lungs erupted in a huge guffaw.

"Bffff. Are you thinking I am going to disappear? Oh...."

He shook his head, untangling his limbs from mine. He strutted across the floor, ambivalent to his own nakedness, and plucked up his white suit jacket. He pulled his wallet from a pocket, and from that he slipped out a business card. He displayed it for me.

"Ma carte," he stated, before slipping it into my tiny night bag on the floor.

I pretended not to care, but I was buzzing.

I watched him from where my head rested in my hands, growing cosier on the empty bed. I yawned.

He laughed. He fitted himself in beside me on the bed, completely relaxed. I snuggled against him and let my eyes drift closed. The distant sounds of the harbour below faded and I sank into a safe soft sleep.

Chapter 16

The sweet touch of Xavier's hand accompanied the sounds of Praia when they drifted back. I could have lain here all afternoon, letting the warm sea air waft across me in this beautiful secret space, but there couldn't be much time left.

I sat up, looking for Xavier's watch. He drew me back down and assured me we had time to spare.

"You would like a shower before we go, perhaps?"

"There's a shower here?" I looked around. I had not seen one but it seemed logical there would be something given the way Xavier's brother and his wife-to-be had used the room before. Before they had been cruelly…

Xavier led me down a short hallway leading off a corner of the room. The white finish of the walls had rendered the gap somewhat invisible in the bouncing light of the room. A little ways in, the hallway opened up into a white tiled room with a working toilet and a large tiled basin. The basin was essentially a tub with steps to one side—large enough for two people to stand or sit in comfortably. A very wide showerhead protruded from the corner above the basin, promising to deliver water that felt like rain. A high window above the shower contributed a similar ethereal glow to the room's larger counterpart. Someone had even left us a cloth, some soap, and a bath towel in a basket by the toilet.

"I think that the bath towel is for you," observed Xavier as he turned on the tap and the shower burst to life with clean warm water. He stepped over the edge of the tub into the shower. His look acknowledged acceptance of the subtle dig that had presumably been aimed at him.

"Well, I might be convinced to share it," I teased, grabbing the cloth and soap and stepping in after him. The water that poured over me cleansed me clear to my soul.

We washed each other with a tenderness we would not have reserved for ourselves. We were still exploring. And memorizing. And leaving a trail behind.

Xavier let the soap and the cloth go somewhere behind us when he finished washing my back so that he could wrap his hands around me and explore my front. He licked the water off the back of my neck. I reached up to caress his face. His cast-bound hand met mine and grasped my fingers in his own. He pressed our hands against the cool tile wall and held me close to him with the other. He buried his face into my neck.

He held me to him so long I had to wriggle myself free. I turned to look at him and swore I could see tears mixed with the water from the shower.

He turned away when he saw me notice, and stepped out to grab the towel for both of us.

We dried off and got dressed. I took advantage of the opportunity to change my clothes, which Xavier found amusing. I was relieved that he made no mention of their poor fit.

Our taxi driver was waiting with the car when we emerged from the misfit ruin of the house. He checked his watch when he saw us, but did not appear hard pressed. We had nothing in the way of luggage—just my tiny carry-on which I brought with me into the back seat. The driver kept spying on us through the rear-view mirror during the drive to the airport. He may have thought something was wrong given how quiet we were.

Xavier and I held hands below the driver's intrusive sight line, and looked out the windows on our separate sides of the cab. I could still feel Xavier's presence inside me. I regretted that the sensation would be gone by the end of the day.

We travelled across the top of the small city, blessed with breathtaking views of the African Atlantic. The taxi altered course to plunge down a steep incline through a parade of colourful Colonial buildings closer to the centre of town. We drove through a market area full of empty stalls and piled boxes. The day was coming to a close. We arrived at the industrial area surrounding the airport too quickly for our taste but its wide unused spaces, ugly buildings, and sparse hand-painted advertising granted us an excuse to want to go.

Xavier jumped out of the taxi the moment it pulled up at the departure drop-off. He strode around the car and opened the door for me, handing the driver a large wad of bills while I climbed out of the taxi. I looked around and saw that we were being scrutinized by a number of men, all scattered in different locations and all wearing sunglasses.

"I think we're being watched," I warned Xavier, as we headed into the terminal arm in arm.

"I am certain that we are being watched," he replied. "Mercado will be sure I am on the next plane out of here."

"Aren't I on the next plane out of here?"

"You are flying to another island. I have to leave the country. It's ok; I don't want to stay."

We passed through security exceptionally fast. I was glad Xavier was able to accompany me right to the gate. I savoured his presence, memorizing every last second of his touch, his smell. His being with me shielded me against any thoughts of further danger. I wasn't sure that any further dangers would happen at this point, but regardless...

The plane was already at the gate when we arrived. Boarding hadn't begun, but it was time to say our goodbyes. I took a deep breath, fighting back the tears that pushed to get out.

"Your uncle should be waiting for you, I think," he said, interrupting my farewell. "And there is something that you should know before you speak with him."

My shoulders drooped. What could he say that would surprise me now?

"Someone at Mindelo has told him that you were held up at security here and that is why you missed the connection," he continued. "If he asks. I am hoping that he will be there to meet you for the later flight. There will be a taxi for you if he is not. A friendly taxi."

"Why didn't you tell me that earlier?" I snapped. "Or

better—let me have some input on whatever lie you want to tell my uncle?"

He looked stunned by my angry response.

"Everything was happening very quickly. There was not time to explain," he said, hurt.

"There was lots of time to explain since then. You could have told me any time this afternoon."

"I was enjoying my time with you too much. But it will be ok—it is better that they do not know the real reason for the delay."

"I'm tired of all this lying!"

"You are right—I should have told you. Much of what has happened I did not know myself. It was selfish of me to want to hide what I did know. I am ashamed of my past here, and of the debt I have owed to Mercado since he lost his daughter. It is not easy to talk about."

He tried to take my hand but I wouldn't let him. This was ruining our goodbye.

The airline flight attendants unlocked the door to the tarmac as a doubtful-looking bus pulled up, and the handful of passengers began lining up with their tickets ready.

"I can tell you," he continued, "that when I spoke to Mercado from Paris and told him that I had failed an opportunity to deliver his prize, I also told him that my attempt had put someone else, another man's daughter, in danger. He called me many names. And he threatened many bad ends and he hung up the phone. But he called later to tell me that I would want to be on the next plane leaving from Dakar to Praia, that there would be a car waiting when I landed, and that I would want to be certain that "he" was following. I did not have to ask who he was talking about or what he was planning."

"You were planning on staying in Paris, otherwise?" Maybe my first instincts had been correct.

"Are you crazy?" he cried. "Alicia kept me informed about your flight plans, and I had already purchased my airplane ticket when Mercado called me back. I was very happy that I would be able to land with you in Praia without being shot in the head."

"*With* me? I had no idea you were on my flight! Why not sit with me? Why leave me alone and terrified?"

"That was Mercado's plan. I only agreed because I knew that Mercado's pride would keep you safe—he would be sure you came to no harm. If I did what he wanted I would both repay my debt to him and make a stop to Scarab's threat to you. And Mercado had to have it his way. I hated that he would put you through that fear, but I could say nothing to change his mind. I was furious. I *am* furious. And I do not want to tell your family. How can I ever face your family if they know I have put you in such danger? How am I able to face you?"

He looked down at his feet, then away. He was not used to having to apologize. He had spent so much of his life protecting others on his own terms that perhaps the habit was hard to break.

"I don't want to fight," he pleaded, turning back to me. His eyes were raw.

"You used me as *bait*," I pointed out. His reluctant tears might be the only apology I would ever get from him. Was that good enough for me? What kind of respect for me did that demonstrate? And if I accepted his excuse as an apology, what did that say about the kind of respect I had for myself?

"I'm not another one of your stray dogs," I said. "I don't need to be looked after like that—or told what to do. I should have been part of *all* these decisions. The whole way along."

The announcement of last call for my flight cut through our painful argument.

He gripped my face in his slender hands and kissed me one last time. I didn't fight his kiss, which lingered until an insistent flight attendant plucked at my sleeve.

I held his gaze through the final boarding gate, and as far out onto the tarmac as I could despite the danger of tripping. The bus to the waiting plane honked, and someone else shouted at me between blasts. I could still feel the pressure of his lips on mine as the bus door shut behind me, cutting off my last sight of him. I doubted I would ever see him again.

Chapter 17

I found Bill waiting for me at the Mindelo airport as Xavier hoped. Margaret had gone back to the boat to make dinner. I was told I should be prepared for some serious comfort food. Bill didn't ask me many questions—just whether I was in good health, and how hungry I was.

Margaret served homemade chili full of fresh vegetables she had bought at the Mindelo market that morning in anticipation of my return, topped with the last of her good cheddar from the Canaries. Bill opened a bottle of wine.

I listened with a glad heart to their tales of quiet seas and short-wave radio jokes, but shared none of my own stories. I wasn't ready to yet. My exhaustion stole my courage. I excused myself early and slept for twelve hours straight.

Quixotic departed Mindelo early the next morning. A host of dolphins leapt around the boat in farewell as the Cape Verdes shrank behind us. The Atlantic crossing seemed tame, relative to all that led up to it. The gauntlet of storms and a recurring rip in the main sail were nothing like the troubles I'd been through.

Neither Bill nor Margaret believed the "floated to the shore of Africa" story, but I never divulged any alternative explanation. And while they accepted the cause I gave for the boat's explosion, they were quick to condemn Xavier for being careless with his propane.

As I described the care that Xavier had taken following the explosion (with certain details strategically omitted), I learned two important things: One, on hearing that their beloved niece had been in the hands of a careful man who had pushed himself to his physical limits and pulled diplomatic strings at a foreign embassy to ensure her safety, my aunt and uncle conceded that accidents sometimes happen and that maybe Xavier was not in fact responsible for blowing up his own boat and its precious cargo; and two, on telling of how that gorgeous man had done those things in order to keep me from harm, it finally sank in that he had fallen in love with me, and that I had fallen in love with him, too.

I took Xavier's his business card from its shrine at the end of my cabin bunk and put it away in my luggage in a safe spot where it wouldn't get damaged. Xavier Perren—I had his full name now, too. I promised myself that once I returned home— likely to my parents' basement, but one could only move up from there—and landed the decent job that I now felt I was capable of, I would be ready to reach out to Xavier on my own terms.

I deeply regretted not accepting his attempt at an apology. Would he accept mine when the time came? Would it matter by then?

***

Dawn broke softly on the last day of our sail. The pale gray silhouette of an island peered from the thin haze of the horizon, barely visible. The sky itself grew a brighter, deeper blue as the sun rose behind us in the east, the details of the island of Antigua becoming crisper with each passing hour.

Margaret and I drank our coffee in the cramped (compared to *Orion*'s) cockpit, musing about how we'd like to spend whatever time remained of the day once we'd docked safely and secured the boat. Margaret wanted to wander up to the Marina proper and investigate the shop situation. I suggested we all go, and maybe we would find a nice tropical café with a patio overlooking the ocean we'd sailed. Bill climbed up from the galley below and reminded Margaret and me that before anyone went anywhere we had to check in with immigration and get our passports stamped. Then he added that a café with a view would be just the thing.

I took the wheel after breakfast, steering the yacht ever

closer to the island ahead. Tiny blocks of white washed buildings were now visible against the lush tropical green of the trees. The single bumpy line of gray transformed into a series of hills—former volcanos—that composed the heart of the island. A loose collection of billowy clouds hung over the landmass like a floating hat.

Bill announced that we were close enough to raise the Antiguan flag on *Quixotic*'s mast. Bill kept all his flags in a plastic shopping bag under one of the benches in the cockpit, so it took a few minutes to sort out which flag to put up. When he found the right one—a golden sun over a blue ocean rising between two red hills on a black sky—he posed with it so Margaret could take his picture.

After the flag was up, Bill called ahead to the Marina he'd reserved for *Quixotic* to let them know our estimated arrival time. We were still a couple of hours out, and needed to sail around the south end of the island in order to reach the Marina's sheltering bay. The Marina harbour master warned Bill to carefully follow the buoy channels into the bay or risk running aground. He added that immigration had a convenient check-in shack on the grounds, but that the staff kept short hours.

Bill took over the remainder of the sail. Margaret and I sat in the cockpit, enjoying the view, interrupted by the occasional command from Bill. As we rounded the south end of Antigua a rainbow formed under the clouds.

Bill's anxiety rose the closer we got to the forewarned shallow bay, and became worse once we were through it and motoring between expensive yachts in the marina, preparing to dock. But both Margaret and I took the barks in stride—they weren't personal, and we were both confident in our preparedness. Fenders in position, the boat drifted at an easy glide (slower than a stroll), her lines untangled for a quick tie-up to the dock. We were ready to jump onto the dock and catch the yacht as she slid into place.

A few people milled around near our destined slip. Bill shouted ahead to ask for help catching the boat as we manoeuvred her. He had to reverse the boat into the slip, something he hated doing. The boat never seemed to move in the direction Bill expected it to. One or two of those on the dock jumped in to help. One in particular looked very familiar. I knew those tall, slender limbs anywhere.

What the hell was he doing here?

I fought the imposition of my pounding heart as I straddled the lifeline before hopping ashore onto the dock. I wanted to look at him but if I turned away from my task I would mess up and I didn't want to risk that. I jumped at the right time, landed smoothly, and put my hands out to catch the rail as the boat continued towards me. My hands, however, coated in panic-sweat, slid uselessly along the rail without impeding the boat's momentum.

"Oh, shit," I said.

"Hey!" shouted Bill.

"Merde," said Xavier, catching the boat just before it rammed into the dock.

I stared at him now, with his short hair a hint longer, his white linen suit replaced by a different pair of loose shorts, the bruises almost completely faded from his tanned, bare chest. His hand remained in a cast, however, and he looked to me to help him tie off the boat with my two working ones.

"What are you doing here?" I whispered as I knelt beside him to tie the lines, my heart thumping in my ears.

"You forgot to give me your phone number," he shrugged. He wore a deadpan expression but couldn't hide the twinkle in those blue eyes. There was something else, too. He wouldn't hold my gaze, and his normally smooth grace seemed oddly jittery. Then I got it—he was actually nervous.

Bill interrupted my light-bulb moment to insist that he and Margaret and I get to customs and immigration before the place closed. I left Bill to politely greet Xavier and thank him for the help in docking *Quixotic* while I retrieved my relevant paperwork.

Two hours later, Xavier and I got a chance to escape together to a shaded bench overlooking the water. We held hands while Xavier got up the nerve to speak.

"After you left," he said. "I felt very much stung by your

words. But the more I licked my wounds the more I tasted the truth of them. I knew… I knew that I needed to tell you how much. And I am afraid that to say sorry does not come close to how I feel. But I am sorry. I am sorry that I didn't tell you what was happening, and that my actions made you feel more scared. I don't know why I felt that was the right thing to do, and probably that does not matter. What matters is that you know that I have heard what you said. And if… If…" He stopped and looked at me and there was fear in his eyes.

"You *love* me," I said, as if it were an accusation.

"Yes, of course," he said, as if I should have known all along. "But that is not the question. The question is how do you feel? About me?"

"Oh…," I said, looking at him and seeing an adolescent boy asking the girl he really likes out on a first date. This was that moment. What I answered could either crush his spirit or open me to a whole new experience. I could stick to my existing plan, to wait for an unknown indefinite future of self-determination, knowing I wanted to be with him anyway, or I could be self-determining right now, and grasp this unbelievable future being offered to me.

"You love *me*," he said, mimicking me. And saving me from the insipid *I love you, too*.

"Yes," I said. "You fucking blow me away."

"Well," he said through the laughter of his relief, "Maybe we can make plans together, then. Because… I have not. I have made no plans. Rien."

I burst out laughing with him.

"I do love you," I said. "And when you're ready to go home to Paris I'm coming with you. For good. As long as we fly— I think I'm done sailing with you for a while."

"Is tomorrow too soon?" he giggled. "Or now?"

He kissed me through our laughter—the sweet first kiss of the rest of our lives.

Fin

ABOUT THE AUTHOR

Agnès de Savigny has lived and worked in England, Canada, France, and Mexico.

She has travelled to every continent except Antarctica, and dipped her toes in every ocean except the Arctic.

Her casual adventures have taken her sailing across both the Atlantic and Indian oceans, horseback riding on the beach in New Zealand with a hot cowboy, salsa dancing in Granada with a hot Venezuelan instructor, and playing drums in Zanzibar with a group of hot musicians.

She has flirted around the globe.

When not gallivanting around the world or making up stories about tortured romantic souls, she can be found at home cuddling with kittens and/or her sweetheart.

She is currently working on her next novel. Please look for her on Facebook or Amazon.com.

www.ingramcontent.com/pod-product-compliance
Lightning Source LLC
Chambersburg PA
CBHW020126180626
46810CB00004B/1423